For Lou Ellen,
a true friend

The
FORETELLING

Caroline Crane

DODD, MEAD & COMPANY
NEW YORK

1 2 3 4 5 6 7 8 9 10

Library of Congress Cataloging in Publication Data

Crane, Caroline.
  The foretelling.

  I. Title.
PS3553.R2695F6   813'.54   82-1409
ISBN 0-396-08056-1   AACR2

FS

The
FORETELLING

Also by Caroline Crane

WIFE FOUND SLAIN
COAST OF FEAR
THE GIRLS ARE MISSING
SUMMER GIRL

Angela

At night, sometimes, I dream of Burley's Falls and the people who lived there. And died there.

The dream is a frightening one of lakes and rivers. I am engulfed in inky water. How I got there, I can't remember. I have no past, no future, no meaning. I am only a consciousness, drifting in time.

Objects float past me—tree trunks, fantastically long ones with their branches cut off. They make me think of the hemlocks at the bottom of Mile Gorge. I can still see those hemlocks, their tips far below me. The sight of it makes me sick.

I am stricken with panic and want to escape. What else is in the water? What horrid things down near my feet? I hate deep water, not only because I am afraid of drowning, but because of the things that might be in it.

Am I alone? No, there is someone else. David Bennett swims toward me. He passes quite close by without noticing me. And then Marcia Wollsey. I am surprised to see Marcia again. I want to call to her and tell her how glad I am that she is not hurt after all. My voice makes no sound.

Everywhere I look, I see nothing but water. It seems to cover the whole world. Once I predicted that I would drown someday. And yet, in the dream, I am not drowning. I am only there.

A rowboat mysteriously appears. My brother, Tom, is rowing a boatload of children. I look to see if mine are with him. Yes, they are safe. They sit quietly in the boat like wooden dolls, and then they are gone, vanished into the night.

Where are the other people I knew? Ross Giordano? Betty Meeker? Zinnia? My mother?

And Glen. How could I have forgotten? Glen!

The dream is gone. I wake in a dark room, which gradually becomes familiar to me. My room. Ours. I have a hard time coming back from Burley's Falls. A hard time realizing that all that is past and some of those people are dead. Now I know what they mean by the expression "sleeping like a log." I must not have moved for hours. The dream has sat upon me, crushing me, like the mythical Night Mare.

Was it really a dream? I look beside me. Yes, he is there. I can see only the dark of his hair on the pillow. He is lying with his back to me. I move over so that I am resting against him. He stirs in his sleep.

For a long time I lie awake, thinking. It was nothing but a dream. Yet it brings back memories and makes them vivid. Memories of things that really happened. Events I can never forget, but which I would rather not relive.

The terrible part about it is some of those things might have happened because of me. At least it seemed so at the time. But who knows? Maybe I was only an observer, seeing the future that was bound to unfold.

Or maybe it was what I saw, and what I said, that made it unfold the way it did. I will never know.

1

Looking back on the memories awakened by her dream, and the part she had played in those events, Angela thought she could pinpoint the exact moment when it all began.

It was the middle of October. She remembered that she had spent the afternoon typing a long report, and her back ached. She paused, resting her arm across her typewriter, and gazed out of the window at the wild Catskill autumn.

The trees and mountains were bright with color, glowing red and yellow against a charcoal sky. Clouds of lighter gray seethed with the wind. In the midst of so much boiling gloom, the headquarters of the Fabian Construction Company seemed a separate, enclosed little world.

From around a plastic partition at the end of the corridor, she heard Mrs. Oudhousen laugh. Then came the indistinct murmur of old Tony Fabian's voice. They had been together for nearly an hour. Mrs. Oudhousen laughed again, a polite, departing chuckle. Her shadow rose, distorted through the plastic. She emerged from Mr. Fabian's office and sailed toward Angela.

"Guess what. We've done it!"

"We have?" Angela eyed the large plastic handbag that had come to rest on her typed report. "What have we done?"

"Burley's Falls," said Mrs. Oudhousen, "is getting what

it's always needed. Actually, it's a combination of things, all in one village center. The part I hooked him on is a volunteer emergency squad."

"For Burley's Falls?" It hardly seemed necessary. Burley's Falls had a resident population of 387, and there was a good hospital nearby in Kaaterskill.

"For the area," Mrs. Oudhousen explained, "and that means Mile Gorge Park and the road down the mountain. You know how often accidents happen on that road. And remember last year when a guest at Villa Castelli had a heart attack, and the ambulance from Kaaterskill couldn't get there in time?"

Angela remembered. Her own mother, who worked at Villa Castelli, had been there when it happened.

"And then," continued Mrs. Oudhousen, "my pet project. A free reading room."

"A library? For Burley's Falls?"

"Just a small one. I always felt it would be a good idea. The library in Kaaterskill is too far away for people to bother."

Mrs. Oudhousen went on to describe her project. It was to be in the Wingate House, over near La Suisse Restaurant. The house had been vacant since May and was now for sale. Mr. Fabian had offered to match any funds raised by the village toward its purchase and the founding of the various facilities.

"I really wanted the library," she confessed. "It will give me something to do, now that I've retired. And I think the emergency squad is needed, especially if we can get some paramedic training for them."

She planned to start her fund raising with a carnival and dance, to be held in Central High School in Kaaterskill, where she had been librarian for thirty years, and where her husband still taught. It was the school that served Burley's Falls and other neighboring villages.

A Halloween ball, she decided, since this was October. The committee would be meeting at her house that evening, and she invited Angela to join them.

Angela noticed Glen Fabian watching from the doorway of his office. After Mrs. Oudhousen left, he came over to her desk.

"What was that all about?" he asked.

"I should think you'd know, if your family's in on it," she said. "Burley's Falls is going to be upgraded."

"Is it really? How?"

She told him, although he would hear it soon enough from his grandfather, Tony Fabian.

Glen, barely thirty, was the third generation in the current leadership of his family's company. Directly above him were two uncles and his father, Michael, who was Angela's immediate boss.

"She's not letting any grass grow, is she?" he remarked when Angela mentioned the meeting that night.

"Not Mrs. Oudhousen. She probably wants to get started before we're snowed in."

She expected Glen to be involved to some extent, but was unprepared, when she arrived at the meeting, to find him standing by the Oudhousen fireplace, drinking a cup of coffee.

"Just representing the family interests," he explained.

"And we're thrilled to have him here," fluttered one of the women. Glen acknowledged the comment with a rakish smile, then sat down next to Angela, his thigh touching hers.

Mrs. Oudhousen outlined the plans for the dance. It was to include a live orchestra, food and drink, and a series of side attractions. There would be several game booths, a shooting gallery featuring darts instead of bullets, taffy apples, popcorn, cotton candy, a wishing well, and a fortune-teller.

"Who can we get to tell fortunes?" she asked. "Does anybody know tarot cards? Palm reading?"

"There's a woman down the mountain," someone suggested. "Lydia Dawn. Isn't she your grandmother, Angela? I hear she's pretty good at that."

Angela shrank into the sofa cushions as they turned to her expectantly. "But she wouldn't. She just wouldn't. She never goes out of her house."

They were all watching her. She wondered how many of them had guessed that her grandmother was the eccentric old recluse who lived by the roadside in a ramshackle cabin overrun with chickens.

"Well, then," said Mrs. Oudhousen, "how about yourself? You must have inherited some talent. Actually all you need is dramatic abil—"

"I second it!" Glen said. "You'd be great, Angela. You have just the right quality."

"But I—"

"Good, then, that's settled." Mrs. Oudhousen beamed and proceeded to the selection of a food committee.

By ten-thirty, when the meeting was adjourned, all the jobs had been delegated. Angela walked out alone into the chilly night, thinking that perhaps she had gotten off easily after all. She did not have to decorate the gym, or round up a dance band, or find out where to rent a cotton candy machine. She would only have to sit there and read a few palms.

Running footsteps followed her from the house. "Drive you home?" offered Glen. "I feel some rain." He ushered her into his gray Mercedes and started the engine.

She asked, "Have you ever been to a fortune-teller? What sort of things do they say?"

"I really wouldn't know. Can't you just make up a lot of stuff?"

6

"I could, but it doesn't seem honest."

He laughed. "Is any of it honest?"

"And speaking of fortune-tellers," she continued, "what did you mean when you said I had the right quality for it?"

"A sort of deceptive innocence. Don't you think that's appropriate?"

She did not believe there was anything deceptive about her innocence, but preferred not to let him know it. In any case, they had already covered the short distance to her house. She dashed through the rain, then watched from a window as he bumped his car down the rutted driveway and turned back the way they had come.

The house was silent. Her mother and brother had gone to bed. They had left a light on for her, a solitary lamp burning in an otherwise dark cottage, with rain falling on the roof. She felt, for a moment, unbearably sad.

The moment passed. It had to do with more than the darkness and the rain. It might have been loneliness, and perhaps also the fact that the night of the carnival would be her twenty-first birthday.

She had once planned to spend that evening with Ross Giordano. They had invested three years in each other, and their breakup was a raw, bleeding wound. And now she would be twenty-one, still single, and telling fortunes on her birthday, while everyone else would be part of a couple.

What if Ross was there with another girl? And Glen, who was so attentive sometimes and had driven her home. If he went to the dance at all, it would be with Marcia Wollsey, whose father owned a chain of supermarkets.

She switched off the lamp and groped down the short hallway to her room.

Just before he rounded the bend, Glen looked back and saw the light go off. It hadn't taken her long. He wondered if she was already in bed. He could almost see her there. Probably she wore some god-awful warm nightgown, but he could imagine her any way he wanted. That tall body . . . he liked the bare torso of a statuesque girl. Her dark blond hair would be loose on the pillow, her wide gray eyes dreaming into the darkness.

He turned up the long driveway to his house, toward the lights he could see twinkling among the tree trunks. Now that he was on home territory, his thoughts turned to Marcia. He would probably end up marrying Marcia.

One for a wife, the other for a mistress. If he could have that, he'd have it all. Marcia, the practical, prosaic one, would be an ideal partner. A hostess. An asset.

And Angela? With her, he felt that he could soar.

But it would never happen. She was hooked on that idiot Giordano. And Giordano would kill anybody who poached on his territory.

A pity, Glen thought as he drove into the six-car garage. What could Giordano give her?

2

By the following afternoon, a poster had appeared on the company bulletin board, advertising the carnival. As Angela stood reading it, Zinnia Bennett, the new clerk-typist, came up beside her.

"Are you going?" Zinnia asked.

"I guess so."

"Oh? Who with?"

Zinnia was sounding her out about Ross Giordano. It irritated but did not surprise her. Although volatile and unreliable, Ross was still the best-looking man in Burley's Falls.

"Probably nobody," Angela replied. "I'm telling fortunes."

She went out to the parking lot where her brother, Tom, a Fabian construction worker, waited in his car. He had been asleep, but woke when she opened the door.

"Can we make a slight detour?" she asked. "Just down to Grandma's."

"Detour!" Tom exclaimed. "It's miles out of the way. What for?"

"I need some information. It won't take long"

They headed east on the mountain highway, leaving Kaaterskill and the Fabian offices behind them. Five miles later they reached Burley's Falls, almost on the edge of the Catskill escarpment.

The first house in town was the Bennetts'. Zinnia Bennett was probably following them home even then in her red Camaro. Next, a long driveway, guarded by two blue spruces, led to the Wollseys' stately home with its broad lawns and gardens, its tennis court, its fountain and sun clock.

And high on the mountainside, overlooking the entire village, was the Fabian mansion. Trees hid most of it, but she could see it briefly as a single ray of late sun broke through the clouds to strike a window in a blaze of orange fire. It was the only sunlight in all the sky.

On the eastern side of the village was their own home, a shabby white bungalow set back from the road. Its green shutters were dulled by weather, its wide porch cluttered with sagging rockers and a battered swing.

"You know," said Tom as he drove past it, "fortune-telling is illegal in this state."

"How come?"

"I don't know, but that's what I heard. Predicting the future for pay is illegal. You can do character analysis, but not predictions."

"That's a stupid law. Who'd want their character analyzed? Most people know their own character. Anyhow, it's not for pay, it's charity."

"It's still money," he pointed out.

They followed a road that wound down the mountain, crisscrossing broad streams, hairpin-turning past waterfalls and wild crags, deep cliffs and gorges. The autumn colors were fading into dusk. The evergreens that carpeted the slopes appeared black, and the late afternoon grew colder.

In a sheltered nook by a bend in the road, Lydia Dawn lived alone with her chickens. Her small house, nestled

10

against the mountain, was jerry-built and unpainted. The rest of the nook was occupied by a vegetable patch and a chicken coop. The white leghorns that were usually everywhere, in their yard and out of it, had retired for the night.

Tom knocked on the front door. It opened a crack. "Well, Tom," Lydia said, pulling it wider. She wore her usual jeans and plaid flannel shirt. Her face was unlined, her gray hair pulled back and held by a plastic band.

"Yes, it's us," Tom assured her. "Angela wants to ask you about telling fortunes."

Lydia led them through the kitchen into her small sitting room, where a fire burned in the fireplace. After Angela had explained her errand, Lydia looked from one to the other.

"Well, Tom, what will *you* be doing? Sitting in front of the television? You should get out more."

"I get out plenty," he protested.

"To work and back. You're almost as bad as I am." Turning to Angela, she said, "And you're the opposite. You dream too much and want too much." She took Angela's hand and turned it palm side up. After a moment of study, she shook her head. "He's no good for you."

"Who isn't?" Angela asked.

"No good." Lydia dropped the hand. "It don't matter what I say, you won't listen, but I'm telling you anyway."

"If you mean Ross Giordano, I'm finished with him. Do you really see something?"

"What do you think I'm saying? Now listen, don't hurry it. You just wait. It will all come right, but if you hurry, it won't be right."

"Grandma, please tell me how you do this."

Another shake of the head. "You won't listen to me, I know."

11

"I'll listen if you tell me how you do it." Angela offered her hand again. "Tell me which lines are which. Where's the Heart Line?"

Lydia pointed to the upper of two creases that ran parallel across the palm. Tom fidgeted, glancing at his watch.

"Tom, be patient." Lydia disappeared into the tiny bedroom and returned with a small, thin book, which she handed to her granddaughter. Its cover was green, and so old and faded that the title was barely readable. *A Primer of Palmistry.*

Angela flipped through the pages. "Is this how you learned?"

"That and a few other places." Lydia saw them to the door. "It's all you need to know, right there. And you can keep the book."

She couldn't have learned from a book, Angela thought. Probably she didn't even need to read palms. She just knew things. Or seemed to.

As they drove back up the mountain, Tom asked, "When and where is this great event taking place?"

"Two weeks from Saturday, at Central High. That's not much time, but she wants a Halloween theme."

"If it's at Central, I'm not going. I had enough of that place." He swerved to miss a raccoon crossing the road. "Hey, that's your birthday, isn't it? Can't you think of anything better to do on your birthday?"

"At the moment, no. I wonder who she was talking about when she said 'he' was no good for me."

"Ross. Who else?"

"I told her we broke up."

"Look, that's how they do it, okay? They say something mysterious that could mean anything, and people draw their own conclusions. You went there to learn how to read palms. So now you know."

When they reached their house, Tom turned on the news,

12

which was nearly over, while Angela curled up on her bed to read the book.

Its author was a woman named Cordelia Bedfrey Hunt; the date of publication, 1897.

It began with a description, almost a paean to palmistry.

> *"And receive his mark in his forehead, or in his hand."* *Rev. xiv:9*, it quoted.
>
> *In all the human race, no two characters and no two destinies are alike. In the signs of Cheirosophy (Palmistry) no two hands have ever been found in which the lines, mounts and fingers are the same. The human hand is perfectly marked with the individual's character and his endowments at birth. In the hands we may read how the person has cultivated these talents, or failed to cultivate them.*

Next came a discussion of the shapes of hands. They could be square, spatulate, scientific, or artistic.

She examined her own. According to the book's description, they were artistic.

She raised her head as she heard the television go off. Tom was on his way to the bathroom to take a shower.

Intercepting him, she caught his hand and studied it.

"It's square. Absolutely square. That's amazing, Tom."

"Why is it amazing?"

"Well, it sort of fits you."

"Huh!" He jerked his arm away from her and closed the bathroom door. She went back to her book, guiltily aware that their mother would be home soon and something ought to be done about dinner.

She found page after page, not only on the meaning of hand shapes, but of fingers and mounts as well—a mount, as she discovered, being the pad at the base of a finger.

13

Each shape and each mark, each position of each mark, had a meaning of its own, wrote Mrs. Hunt.

The next chapter dealt with lines. She read about the Head Line, the Heart Line, the Life Line. The Line of Fate and the Line of the Sun. Each line varied from hand to hand, just as destiny varied from human being to human being.

The length of the Head Line, declared Mrs. Hunt, was a gauge of the owner's intelligence. A deeply sloping Head Line meant a great imagination. Too deeply sloping a Head Line might indicate a possible suicide.

Her own Head Line sloped sharply. Enough, according to the book, to show imagination, but not enough for suicide.

Imagination, definitely. She often spun fantasies of attractive men and faraway places. It was the only way to survive the doldrums of Burley's Falls.

The Heart Line was high on her palm. That signaled a passionate and possessive character, one given to unreasonable jealousy. Possibly true. She admitted to feeling resentful of Zinnia's interest in Ross, even though she herself no longer had a claim on him.

It reminded her to look for the Marriage Line. Her own took a sharp turn downward. That, said Mrs. Hunt, meant that her marriage partner would predecease her. Since she had no marriage partner at the moment, the prospect was not unduly disturbing.

Tom had finished his shower and was puttering in the kitchen. Good old practical Tom, concerning himself with dinner. She waited until he had the TV dinners in the oven, and then asked to borrow his hand again.

For a long time she studied it, but could think of nothing to say. The lines were only lines. They seemed to bear no relation to what she had learned in the book.

"It seems a rather uneventful life," she said.

14

Tom agreed. "It seems that way."

"It's a long life. I don't see any great wealth or—"

"Aw, you're no good."

"But you'll have one marriage and two children. Or maybe it's three. I can't tell if all those are real lines."

"Where?" He peered at the edge of his palm, below the last finger, where she indicated the Marriage Line. "You mean all those little things are children?"

"Not all. Just the ones that go up from the line. The others, coming down, mean something, but I can't remember what. Let me check."

Tom frowned uneasily as she opened the book and turned to the chapter on family and children.

" 'Tiny hairlines descending from the Line of Marriage toward the Heart Line,' " she read aloud, " 'foretell of troubles and adversity brought on by ill health, or illness, of the marriage partner.' "

He snatched away his hand. "Go to hell!"

"Tom! You're not going to take this seriously!"

"If you feel that way, then what are you doing it for?"

"Because I can't say no to Mrs. Oudhousen. I still think of her as a teacher."

"Well, you'd better be careful what you tell people. Who invented this stuff, anyway?"

"I don't know, but you're right. Somebody just made it all up, so how can it really mean anything?"

She folded her own hand and watched the lines deepen into creases. That was all they were. Fold lines, and nothing more. It was ridiculous to think they meant anything.

3

Tom drove her to the carnival, then went home to watch a television special. She felt outlandish in the costume Mrs. Oudhousen had found for her: a floor-length skirt patterned in red and yellow zigzags, and ropes of multicolored glass beads.

The gym at Central High School was transformed. Its lighting was dim and dark red. Black ropes swathed the walls, simulating spider webs. Large bats fluttered on wires hung from the ceiling. The band was playing and crowds were beginning to arrive.

A familiar voice said, "Hey, what's this? You came in costume?"

David Bennett, from Burley's Falls. She had known him all her life—mild, blue-eyed, pleasant David. He worked at Fabian as a draftsman. When he joined her for lunch in the company cafeteria, he would talk endlessly of Betty Meeker, who stood beside him now, smiling at Angela, her arm wrapped around David's.

Angela explained about the costume. "It's Mrs. Oudhousen's idea. My whole act is, really."

"Well, it's eye-catching." David reached for Betty and they danced away.

Angela went up a flight of stairs to the restroom on the

mezzanine. It was packed with women from Burley's Falls and Kaaterskill. She stood before a mirror, adjusting her beads.

Zinnia Bennett's reflection appeared in back of hers. "Where'd you get that dress? And the beads! It's wild, I love it! When do you start? Can I be first?"

"Sure, if nobody else is there ahead of you."

Had she come alone? Angela wondered. Or with Ross?

As Zinnia pushed her way out, Marcia Wollsey entered. She smiled vaguely at the crowd and began combing her chestnut hair.

If Marcia was there, it meant Glen was, too. They were a matched pair. Marcia had a thoroughbred air about her, a kind of wealthy gloss. It showed in her manner and in her grooming. The avocado green dress she wore was classic, well cut, and expensive.

It would clash horribly with the red lights, Angela thought. They would turn it to mud.

At the foot of the stairs, Glen stood waiting for his date. He nodded to Angela. She could feel his eyes still on her as she made her way to the row of booths at the end of the gym.

There were six altogether. Hers was the only one with closed curtains. Next to it stood the wishing well, and beside that, the shooting gallery. The others were devoted to food.

Zinnia waited beside the curtain, talking animatedly with Ross. Angela slipped past them, murmuring, "Just give me a minute to set up."

The booth was formed by several India print bedspreads hung from a light wood frame. Inside was a small round table spread with a paisley shawl. Two chairs faced each other across the table. Beside the client's chair stood an old-fashioned floor lamp with delicate iron curlicues. She switched it on.

17

"Okay, Zinnia. One at a time, please."

Zinnia entered, paid the fifty-cent fee, and took her place at the table. Angela stared at the spread-out hands. This was her first real test.

But Zinnia's were easy. She had a high, soft Mount of Venus, the pad at the base of the thumb. It was the mark of a sensual hand, of passions easily aroused and easily changeable.

"That's incredible," Angela said. "Your hand. It's you! It says you'll fall in love a lot. You're passionate. You like men, and love. And easy living."

"Oh, come on," Zinnia laughed. "You don't have to see my hand to know that."

The main lines were clearly marked and undistinguished.

"Your head and heart are in the right place, and you're going to have a nice, long life."

"Uh—what about marriage?"

"I can't tell exactly, but you definitely will get married. Three times, it looks like." Angela showed her the three small lines, adding, "They don't necessarily mean marriage. It could be a strong attachment."

"You mean three love affairs?"

"Serious love affairs or marriage. Here's an interesting one. You have a Line of Intuition. It means—"

Then again, perhaps it was not a Line of Intuition.

"Wait a minute. It's something else. It's a Via—I don't know how to pronounce it. A Via Lasciva."

"What's that?"

"It means—Well, it means the same thing I said before. An interest in love. Actually sex. And passionate dreams, and money. Maybe even drugs. Sometimes these things are a kind of warning."

"Warning about what?" Zinnia's voice was hard. "I never took drugs. That's one thing I never did."

18

"I didn't say you took them. It doesn't necessarily mean that. I'm sorry, Zin, it's just that I didn't have enough time to learn how to do this easily."

"That's okay, I know you meant well. You said I'll have a nice, long life, three gorgeous guys, and loads of fun and games. Not bad. Thanks." Zinnia swung aside the curtain and walked out.

Angela watched her, but had no time to think about what had happened before Ross entered the booth.

His sudden appearance caught her by surprise. She had not imagined that he would take any interest in palm reading. Now they would be alone together and she would have to touch his hands. And Zinnia would be right outside, waiting.

"How's it going, Ross?"

"It's okay. What about you?"

"Well, you can see where I ended up."

He nodded, not even remembering that this was her birthday. She turned away from the hot, dark eyes and uncurled his fingers.

The first thing she noticed was his long Head Line.

"Ross, look at this. It says here you could do a lot more with your life than pump gas."

"Who couldn't?" he said, unimpressed.

"I mean it. A long Head Line shows high intelligence. And you have a Sun Line! That's a very good mark. You could be really successful, if you wanted to be. Look at this finger. The way it's shaped, it means you can have terrific success as a lawyer. And your Sun Line says you could be great in politics."

"Yeah, sure."

"It also means you're supposed to have a sunny disposition," she added.

Both his thumbs were the clubbed kind. She knew it meant something, but could not remember what. She pointed to the Fate Line and talked on, trying to keep his interest.

"I think this means you'll have an eventful life. Or that you'll amount to something. Not everyone has a Fate Line. And it's a long life."

A long Fate Line with a small cross at the end. A long life ending in—death? A cross, she knew, meant different things in different places.

"I'm sorry, there are a couple of things I'll have to look up. I'm pretty sure this is important."

"Forget it, okay?" He took her own hand and briefly compared it with his. Then, with a playful slap on her palm, he stood up. "You're all right, Angela."

As he pulled open the curtain to leave, she saw a sizable crowd waiting outside her booth. The succession of hands seemed to go on forever. After a trio of giggling teenagers, Betty Meeker came in.

"Angela Dawn, how did you ever get into this racket?"

"Bulldozed, how else?" Angela replied.

"I hope you're having fun."

"It's all right." She took Betty's hand and read, "You have a nice Heart Line. There's this fork at the beginning. That means you're a kind, home-loving person and your husband will love you very much."

She turned the hand to its side. "You'll have one marriage, a long and happy one. I can't tell about the child lines. But this—you have a Line of Health with a star in it."

"Good or bad?" Betty asked.

"Well—" She should not have mentioned it. "It might just mean be careful. I think it's some sort of complication in childbirth. Or sterility, but I doubt it."

"Why do you doubt it?"

"Well, after all, this is only your hand."

"Angela, I want to know what it *says*. I want to know everything."

20

"All about the hearts and flowers and tall, dark men?"

"That's not there, is it? I want to know what it really says. What's the sense in telling me anything if it isn't the truth?"

Angela looked down at the hand. Tell her the truth, or tell her something pleasant? She had never been a good liar.

"I see an early marriage—"

"You said that already. There's something bad, and you won't tell me."

"It's not bad, really. Just these breaks and chains in your Head Line. That means some kind of emotional trouble. And this little line cutting across it. An injury to the head and neck. It's nothing fatal, only—"

For the first time, she was seeing a Life Line that was not long. And worse, the Head Line sloped badly. It ended deep down on the Mount of Luna. The suicide hand.

Betty grew impatient. "What? Come on, tell me."

"You'll pull out of it after a while," Angela invented. "Remember, this is only what might be. But if you take care of yourself—"

"That's not what it says, is it? *I want to know what it says.*"

She could see through all the hedging, and Angela was shocked by her intensity.

Betty repeated, "Tell me what it says, I have to know."

"Well—" If she had to know, maybe it was better to tell her than allow her to guess. "It looks as if you'll have a series of nervous breakdowns. Mental illness or depression, and then—then it will get so bad you might try to take your own life."

And perhaps succeed. Betty's face remained impassive. Finally she said, "To be forewarned is to be forearmed. That's why I wanted to know."

"Betty, you caught me off balance, insisting like that. I

did the same thing to somebody else, telling her she was going to lead a wild life of drugs and men, because I didn't have time to think. But now, really, you're not going to believe this, are you?"

Betty stood up to leave. She was smiling faintly, almost absentmindedly. She does believe it, Angela thought, but before she could say anything, Betty had gone and David Bennett was ducking his tall frame under the bar that held up the front curtain.

Still thinking of the episode with Betty, Angela found it hard to concentrate, and at first saw little to say about his hand.

"You're a very active person." That, because of the wide space between the start of his Head Line and Life Line. "Very restless."

It didn't sound like David.

"You're brave, too. You take chances without even thinking. You'd do well in the military. Or in police work, like your dad."

A gleam of amusement played across his face. "Where's it say that?"

"You have a star on the Mount of Mars." She showed him the pad at the palm's outer edge. "It means honor in military life. Or maybe, as I said, law enforcement. It could apply to anything like that. But don't go changing jobs. Oh, David, do you see this little square?" She pointed to a mark just below the star. "This is a very lucky sign. A Square of Protection. It means you can come through any dangerous situation without being hurt."

He gave a soft whistle and leaned forward. "Is that right? Does this stuff really work?"

"I don't see how it could. But it's funny, the things about people's personalities. A lot of them are true. I don't know why. But the destiny part I just can't swallow."

22

David studied the tiny square, then looked up and grinned. "Well, that's very interesting. I'll see you, Angela." With that, he left.

She heard the clink of a coin in the wishing well next door. She could smell the candied apples, three booths away. The night seemed a dream of eerie red lights, pounding music, and countless hands. She could not leave her booth with that line of waiting hands, but she was becoming unbearably thirsty.

As though he could read her mind, Glen Fabian came in, bringing her a cup of punch.

"Still at it?" he asked.

"Still at it. When are you taking your turn?"

"As soon as I can get Marcia in here. She says she doesn't believe in this stuff, but what the hell?"

As he went out, she saw that the waiting line had shrunk. She wondered how many fortunes she had told. After they counted the money, she would know.

She was suppressing a yawn when Glen came in again.

"I got Marcia talked into it, but you can start with me." He sat down and held out a half dollar. "Cross your hand with silver?"

"That's not real silver," she remarked as, with the coin, he made a sign of a cross over her palm.

"Then maybe it won't work. It's supposed to ward off the devil." He placed his hands on the table. "All right, let's hear the worst."

Glen had a strong, squarish hand. The Mount of Jupiter, below the index finger, was well developed. The finger itself, slightly bent, was fully as long as the middle finger next to it.

"I suppose you know you have an unusual hand," she told him.

"Unusual? How?"

"Look at your finger. This one, the finger of Jupiter. Look how long it is."

"What does that mean?"

"It means you're a born leader. It says you have ambition and pride. I suppose that means you believe in yourself."

"Sounds likely." He regarded his palm with detached interest.

"And this mount, right under it. When it's well padded, like yours, it means the same thing. Ambition and the ability to succeed. Oh, wait."

She moved his hand closer to the light. "You have a star right there. I think it's a star. That's very good. It means honor and power. Ambition gratified. Triumph. From these lines over here, I'd say you'll have great success in business." Which, after all, was his field. "Brilliant, early success. You'll be running the business before you're thirty-five. And with that finger, and everything else, you'll be a king."

He laughed. "King of what?"

"The top of the heap, I guess."

He turned over his hand, admiring both sides. "This is better than I thought. Too bad I don't believe in it, but keep going."

"Well, you have a Sun Line. That's very good. I've only seen one other, and that was on a person you'd never expect."

"Tell me what a Sun Line is."

"It's this thing, that runs up your Sun finger, the fourth one. It more or less means that fortune smiles on you. And your particular Sun Line says you'd do very well in politics."

Ross's had said that, too. But on Ross, it was probably wasted.

Glen's Head Line rose upward, crowding the Line of the Heart until it actually merged with it.

"Your head," she told him, "rules your heart. Whatever

you do is carefully thought out. You're not influenced by emotion."

On closer examination she saw that directly under the second finger, the Heart Line broke in two and then continued. A broken Heart Line. What could it mean? Heart trouble? A heart attack, maybe. She would not mention it.

"With that strong index finger, and your Fate Line and Sun Line ," she concluded, "it looks as if you can go as far as you care to go. You can have all the power, or position, or money that you want."

"Power," he repeated thoughtfully. "What kind of power? Political? Business?"

"Influence, I suppose. Whatever you go into."

She had thought she was finished, but he made no move to leave. His hand remained in hers. She stared intently at it, to keep from looking into his face.

"Another star!" She pointed to the Mount of Venus. "With a line going down from it. I can't remember. Want me to look it up and let you know? They mean different things, depending on where they are, but it's usually something good. You have a very lucky hand."

"And you," he said, patting her cheek, "tell a very nice fortune."

He was gone. Marcia Wollsey came in next, laughing over her shoulder. She was still laughing when she spoke.

"I don't know what you told Glen, but it must have been impressive. Can you do a good one for me, too?" She placed her hand on the table.

The lamplight reflected on her smooth, shiny hair. The clear brown eyes, smiling into Angela's, radiated her perpetual confidence.

Angela looked down at the hands.

"You have a good Sun Line. Both of you have strong Sun

Lines, you and Glen. It means success."

"At anything in particular?" Marcia asked.

"At life. Whatever you decide to do, you'll be successful. It's a good sign to have."

Marcia ducked her head self-deprecatingly. "What else?"

"You have a good Head Line. That's a sign of intelligence. A nice long life. But . . ."

Her Life Line was long, but her Fate Line was very short. Angela remembered that the Fate Line was a time gauge for the events of life. It could be marked off in years. The point at which it crossed the Head Line was supposed to be the thirty-fifth year. Marcia's Fate Line did not reach her Head Line, but ran only a little more than halfway toward it.

"Well? You were starting to tell me something."

"A long Life Line," Angela repeated. Her eyes swept over the rest of the hand. Against her will, they returned to the Fate Line.

"Your Heart Line," she said. "It's a nice one." Like Betty Meeker's, it began with a wide fork. "It shows you're a warm, home-loving person. You have a lot of love to give, and someone will love you very much."

"Mmm," purred Marcia. "I wish you could tell me who."

"Sorry, I can't. Maybe it's Glen, but that's only a guess."

The Marriage Line—it was a short groove, not a real line. There were no children.

"I see . . ."

She could not put into words what she saw. She looked at the palm, lying before her on the paisley tablecloth. It was as though she and Marcia were on an island, in a bubble of light from the lamp. The rest of the world was lost to them somewhere out in the blood-red gloom of the gym.

The music stopped, and she could hear Marcia breathing.

Somehow, it reassured her. She felt the life, the warmth from across the table, the living presence of a human being. That life was a reality. It had to be, for in the hand, she saw death.

The Head Line was broken in two, just under the second finger. The break was small, and after it the line continued, but she remembered the paragraph in her book.

A break in the Head Line under the finger of Saturn, in both hands, is a sign of sudden, early fatality.

Gently she raised Marcia's left hand to the light. The break was there, too.

I'm crazy, she thought. These were nothing but the fold lines in a hand. All the fortunes she had told were only that. They could not predict the future. There was no way a hand, or anything else, could know what might someday happen.

"It seems a very good hand," she said. "A long Life Line, a long Head Line. A Sun Line. You have everything going for you."

Everything except life itself.

"Is it as good as Glen's?" Marcia asked.

"His is spectacular. You'd better hang onto him."

Marcia left the booth, pleased with her good fortune. Angela pondered what she had seen. It was only a line. Just a line with a break in it, which meant nothing. She wished she had never read the book. Tom was right. She would have been better off inventing the whole thing.

Still, she found herself feeling oddly sorry for Marcia, and perhaps a little guilty, knowing what was there.

At midnight, the music ended. The booths were closed and she was free, but the evening was not yet over. Mr.

27

Oudhousen, a small, bouncy man with an artificial pink carnation in his lapel, took charge of the festivities.

"All join hands," he directed.

They took each other's hands, forming a long line. Mr. Oudhousen led them in a snake dance around the gym, then out into the hall, past the library, around the lunchroom and up the stairs.

They danced through the building, over two hundred people, in a great, shuffling snake. The shuffling, Angela found, was strangely hypnotic. The hallways were dim, lit only by night lights. In the shadows she could see the faces of her friends: Zinnia, giggling wildly; Betty and David, laughing together. Even Ross was dancing, his face as darkly somber as ever. Glen, next to Mr. Oudhousen, looked youthful and triumphant, shining with his own charismatic glitter. And holding his hand was Marcia, smiling self-consciously.

Over and over again as the snake coiled around, Angela found herself drawn back to Marcia. It wasn't true, what that break predicted. Of course it wasn't true. But she could not help feeling that she had a terrible secret, something Marcia herself did not know. It was sickening and sad.

And absurd. Marcia was young, with most of her life ahead of her. It made no sense that such a grim destiny could already be fixed, perhaps even at her birth.

And yet, for Angela, it held a dreadful fascination.

4

A long first finger indicates great pride, ambition, and desire for power. Such a person is well endowed with the qualities of leadership. A first, or Jupiter, finger which is longer than the second, or Saturn, finger, is rare, and shows a tyrannical disposition. It is the mark of one with a great desire to rule. Napoleon Bonaparte had such a finger.

She had slept only four hours and was now wide awake, reviewing her book and thinking of the night before. Why had she said those things to Betty and Zinnia? And Glen. She felt silly for what she had told Glen.

Anyway, he was not a tyrant. She supposed it was a matter of degree, and Glen's finger was certainly not as long as Napoleon's.

Outside her room, the sun shone with a wintry brilliance. Her window looked out toward the road and beyond, down the mountainside and up again to the next gray-green ridge.

Across the road, Sal's Service Station had opened at seven o'clock. Ross Giordano, his dark blue jacket zipped against the cold, pumped gas into a van. In the past, he would have waved to her, and sometimes come to the window. Now he did not even bother looking at the house.

She turned to the chapter on markings.

Who would have thought to see a hand with two stars? Most people did not have any. Most people were ordinary mortals with dull hands and dull fortunes. But Glen had two stars.

The stars on the Mount of Venus were many and complicated. Often their connection with a line was important. Glen's had a line running from it, she remembered, but could not recall exactly where it began and ended. It had something to do with inheritance.

Coming to her senses, she realized that of course Glen would inherit someday. He belonged to a wealthy family. That, and not his hand, would be the determining factor.

Ross glanced over at her window. He wondered if she was awake yet. Probably not. It had been a late evening. He would not be awake himself, if it wasn't for this damn job.

He might have known she'd pull a propaganda stunt like that about pumping gas. She'd been at him all along. "What about your future?" she used to ask. He would respond, "What future?" This was it, as far as he was concerned. What else was there? A guy like him didn't have a future, just a living. He was perfectly content. But that was why they had broken up.

Zinnia was different. None of this future stuff for her. All she cared about was a roll in the hay, same as him. He should have known her years ago.

He had, in fact. David Bennett's little sister. She had quite a reputation around the high school. Kid stuff, back then, but now that she was out of school, he didn't mind getting in on the action—without any complications about his goddam future.

*   *   *

30

David Bennett had gone for an early-morning walk, something he had rarely done before on a Sunday. He felt a new awareness of the things around him, the leaves and twigs under his feet, the wind in his hair, the sting of the cold on his ears. Dammit, this was living. How could he have spent twenty-one years stuck behind a desk? Well, sixteen, anyway, counting from first grade.

Active. Restless. Brave. Now that he thought about it, he realized it was true. There must be something in that palm-reading stuff after all, something that could uncover the real self under all the crud of convention. It was fantastic.

And time to do something about it.

Power. It was an interesting word. Glen said it again to himself. As pure sound, it wasn't much more than a weak roll of thunder, or the fall of water in a hydroelectric plant. The meaning of the word was what intrigued him.

He turned off his shaver and stared into the mirror. Good morning, Mr. Fabian. His eyes were bluestone gray, a shade lighter than hers. Had she really seen all that in his hand, or was it just a butter-up job?

Not that he believed in it, anyway. You couldn't, with a thing like that.

But he wouldn't have minded if it were true.

Later that morning, Angela went out to the general store to buy a Sunday newspaper. Betty Meeker was at the counter, paying for a loaf of bread.

Betty was the last person she wanted to see. Angela smiled briskly, dropped her money on the counter and started to leave.

Betty caught up with her. "You were good last night, Angela. Where did you learn all that stuff?"

"Out of an old book. It doesn't mean anything, you know. I only wish I'd—"

"Do you still have the book?" Betty asked. "Could I see it sometime?"

Angela hesitated. There were things in the book that she did not want Betty to see, but she could think of no plausible excuse. "Uh—okay, if you promise not to take it seriously. Why don't you come over for lunch?"

While Angela prepared bacon and tomato sandwiches, Betty looked through the book.

"Actually," Angela said, "if you want to believe that book, Marcia Wollsey has a much worse one than you."

"How do you mean?"

"Well, according to the book—and you know it's all just made up, anyway—according to the book, Marcia's going to die. I don't know when, but long before she's thirty-five."

Betty paled. "How do you know, before she's thirty-five?"

Angela turned to the diagram that showed how to tell time on the Fate Line, and explained what she had seen in Marcia's hand.

Betty gave a choked gasp. "You didn't say anything, did you?"

"Of course not. Especially after what I did to you."

"Angela, what if it's true?"

"How could it be? Anything like that—it hasn't any existence until it happens, so how can it be foretold in your hand?"

Betty continued turning the pages. She was almost at the part about the suicide hand. Angela produced a jar of instant coffee.

"Here, put some in your cup. I don't know how much you want." While Betty was occupied, she removed the book and tossed it onto a counter.

Over lunch, they talked about the carnival and the people

who had been there. When the conversation turned again to Marcia, Betty moaned. "Don't remind me. It's so awful. Every time I see her, I'm going to think—"

"You are not. You're going to be rational."

Betty shook her head and stared dismally at the table. "If anything happens to Marcia—if anything happens . . ."

She looked up as Tom entered the kitchen, heading toward the refrigerator. At the sight of her, an odd, pleased expression came over his face.

"Hi, how are you? Nice to see you."

Betty fluttered her lashes. The worried pallor became a glow.

"Hello, Tom. You didn't go last night, did you? Your sister was fantastic."

"That's putting it mildly." Angela stacked the dishes in the sink. "I was fantastically horrible. You were right, Tom, I should have stuck to character analysis."

She turned to find them sitting together at the table. Betty was comparing her hand with Tom's.

Betty smiled apologetically. "I just wanted to see. They look so much alike. Everybody's hands look alike to me."

Gently Tom placed hers on the table. "Stay out of the racket, Betty Meeker, you're too nice a girl. I already warned Angela she's breaking the law." He gave Betty's hand a reassuring pat. "How did it go last night? Did they make a lot of money?"

Betty did not know. He asked about her job at La Suisse Restaurant, and about her family. When it was time for her to leave for work, he offered her a ride.

La Suisse Restaurant was a half a mile away. Tom returned after nearly forty minutes, his cheeks pink from the cold and a faraway look in his eyes.

"What happened?" asked his sister. "Flat tire?"

"We got to talking. Anything wrong with that?"

33

"Talking? To Betty Meeker?" What could they have to talk about? "Tom, she's pretty thick with David Bennett."

"So?" He unbuttoned his jacket. "What's that supposed to mean? You've got some objection if I drive a girl to work on a cold day?"

"Just thought I'd mention it. You know, Betty seems kind of naive. I think she half believes this fortune-telling stuff. That's why she came over, to see the book."

"Why, what kind of fortune did you tell her?"

"A lousy one. I saw something I didn't want to talk about, but she kept asking. So I had to, but I didn't tell her everything."

"Like what?"

"A lot of mental depression, things like that. And you know, it could be possible. She even went into a tailspin over something I told her about somebody else. As if she believed it. Can you imagine?"

"I can imagine people believing it," he said. "A lot of people do. That's why I think you should leave it alone." He turned on the television to watch a football game.

"You'll be glad to know," she answered without thinking, "that I didn't tell her she has the mark of a suicide."

"A *what*?" He whirled to face her. "Now what, for crissake, is the mark of a suicide?"

His vehemence surprised her. She reminded him humbly, "Don't you want to watch your game?"

"I want to know what's the mark of a suicide."

She showed him her own Head Line, explaining how Betty's was. He thought Angela's looked the same, sloping downward.

"Not as much as hers," she said.

"But more than mine," replied Tom. "What does that make you, a semisuicide? And look how long your line is,

34

all the way down to here, with that sunburst thing at the end."

"A star!" Why hadn't she seen it before?

He said, "Call it whatever you want, but you can't tell me it's any different than Betty's hand."

"Of course it is. Stars are a good sign. Glen Fabian has two of them."

She went to the kitchen, found her grandmother's book on the counter, and turned to the chapter on the Head Line. She was still amazed that she had not seen it before. Perhaps it was because the star was not well marked, and took shape only when her hand was folded in a certain way.

A star at the end of the Head Line sloping into the Mount of Luna is a forecast of death by drowning.

She read the words again. The print grew large and blurry and seemed to rise toward her.

An unlucky star. Why hers?

But it wasn't true. How could it be? Death by drowning, high in the mountains, where the rivers were nothing but shallow trout streams?

There was the lake at Mile Gorge Park. If she stayed away from the lake . . .

At least she did not know when it would happen. The worst torture of death was knowing how and when. There was nothing in her Fate Line.

Or was there? She held it up to the light.

The tiniest break, on her right hand. Nothing on her left. That, too, she had missed. Her eyes had seen only the good signs.

A nearly invisible break, just below her thirtieth year.

35

5

She was at her desk on Monday morning when Glen came in from a field trip, his shoulders sprinkled with melting snow from a preseason flurry.

"Back behind the typewriter, I see," he remarked. "I'd never have expected anything so mundane after the other night."

"That wasn't the real me," she explained. "It was a projection of Mrs. Oudhousen's imagination. But while we're on the subject, do you want me to finish yours?"

"Finish my what?"

"Your fortune. There was something I didn't know, remember? I looked it up."

Of course he didn't remember. The whole thing was too trivial for a busy man like Glen. But, obligingly, he offered his hand.

The mark in question was a star near the base of his thumb. The line that ran from it did not quite meet his Sun Line.

"It looks as if you're in luck again," she told him. "This means you'll inherit money. As if that's news. I mean—"

"Angela, you're just what your name implies."

"Not me, Glen, it's all you. I didn't make anything up.

Now we'd better stop this. I don't want to be caught holding hands with you in the office."

The snow flurries were a forecast of the winter to come. It started early and was bitterly cold.

Neither the cold nor the deep snow deterred Mrs. Oudhousen from her fund raising. She staged a fashion show, and then a variety show, and screened a series of rented films. By the end of January, purchase of the house had gone through and one emergency vehicle had been outfitted.

Burley's Falls residents donated their time to remodeling the structure for public use. On one of her days off, Betty Meeker helped lay a vinyl floor. When Tom arrived in the evening, he found her still at work and finished the job with her. It was the beginning of a friendship that grew slowly, with coffee dates, then dinners, and movies at Kaaterskill's only theater. Tom had rarely dated before, and now, for him, it was almost a whirlwind romance. Betty, however, divided her time between Tom and David Bennett.

One Saturday, when Betty was busy at the restaurant, David and Angela joined several others in painting the newly renovated walls. David talked about the forthcoming emergency squad and the times past when it might have been useful.

"I remember," he said, "when your old man—"

He stopped, thinking it might be painful for her to recall her father's death years ago in a road accident.

"Yes," she sighed, "but the way he drank, he must have had it coming. I doubt if even the emergency squad could have helped him in the long run."

"Well, it's still a treacherous road," David said. "The squad'll be useful, but who's going to be around to volunteer for it? Most of us work in Kaaterskill."

"There are people around here," she replied. "And you and I could put in a few weekends, just to be on call. That's all you have to do, is be on call."

"I dunno." He caught a drip that rolled down the wall. "I don't know if I'm going to be here."

"What do you mean? Where else would you be?"

"Every now and then I get to thinking there's an awful lot of world outside Burley's Falls."

"David Bennett, I thought you were rooted to this place."

"You think I want to spend my life in this dog-post dump? The roots are strictly from habit, kid. I want to go somewhere and fly."

"You mean like in an airplane? You never flew in your life."

"Once I did. At the county fair I took a plane ride, all three minutes of it. But flying's something you feel in your bones."

Before she could comment, Mrs. Oudhousen arrived bringing two lithographs, romantic scenes of the Hudson Highlands, which the Fabians had donated.

"For the library," she explained. "Don't you think that will add a classy touch?"

"It'll make up for not having more books," David cracked.

"We'll have books," Mrs. Oudhousen promised. "We'll have to go scouting for them. I thought of making a trip to New York when the weather gets warmer. Maybe all of us should go, all the people who worked on this thing. It would be fun. Not only sightseeing, but I thought we could visit some secondhand bookstores. We'll get more for our money in places like that."

"Sounds great," David said.

Gradually the winds died down, the rains came, and it was spring. The emergency squad had begun to function,

38

and was to be augmented by a second vehicle in time for the tourist season.

Mrs. Oudhousen made final plans for the trip to New York. Eleven people were planning to go. Tom Dawn had been invited, but had refused. Betty, David, and Angela all took a few days' leave from their jobs.

They left from Sal's garage on a Wednesday evening in early May. As the bus pulled out, Angela looked back and saw Ross Giordano watching them. She waved good-bye. After a moment, he lifted his hand and waved back.

It was dark when they reached New York and traveled across town to their hotel. Betty and Angela shared a room on the ninth floor. After dinner and a walk, they stood together looking out of the window.

Angela was ecstatic. "This is the first time in my whole life that I've ever been anywhere. Isn't it gorgeous?"

Betty replied, "I'm homesick."

The next morning Mrs. Oudhousen began her rounds, acquiring catalogs and booklists, while the others went sightseeing. Angela became separated from David and Betty when she wanted to see the United Nations and they did not. She returned to the hotel late in the day. Betty had not yet come back. Exhausted, she took off her shoes and lay down on her bed.

She was roused by an urgent knocking at the door.

"It's Dave. Can I bring Betty in?"

Angela opened the door. He stood with his arm around Betty. She wore a bandage on her forehead and a brace around her neck. A cut under one eye was swelling into a bruise.

"My God, Betty, what did you *do*?"

They helped her onto the bed. David, his face strained, told Angela what had happened.

"We poked around for a while, and we ended up in Chi-

39

natown. I had a map, but we couldn't find the right subway to come back here, so we took a taxi. These cab drivers are maniacs. The guy went through two red lights."

He slammed his forehead with the heel of his hand.

"The second time, we didn't make it. The cross traffic had already started up and a truck ran right into us. It wasn't his fault, it was the taxi. God, it was horrible. It happened so fast."

"I didn't even see it," Betty murmured. "I didn't have time to be scared. It didn't even hurt for a while, and then it started hurting. But the police were nice, weren't they?"

She turned her head away from David. The look she gave Angela was intense, almost panic-stricken. Then she closed her eyes.

"David, I'm awfully tired."

He understood. Angela saw him to the door. As soon as he had gone, Betty sat up.

"Angela, do you remember what you said that night you were telling fortunes?"

"I said a lot of things. What particular thing do you mean?"

"Don't you remember? You said something about an injury to my head and neck. Angela, *it's happened*."

She sat rigidly, unmindful of her pain. Damn, thought Angela. Betty had been too serious about the whole thing, right from the start. She saw this as the beginning of all the horrors that had been predicted for her.

"For crissake, Betty, anybody can have an accident. Don't you see? It was only because you couldn't find the subway, and that particular taxi happened to come along, and that particular truck happened to be at the intersection—"

"Of course. Because it was meant to be that way. It was all set up, and it came true. And the rest—"

"Tomorrow," Angela said, "when your head feels better, you're going to realize how silly you're being."

But it frightened her—not the possible truth of her prediction, but Betty's reaction to it. And it was her own fault. In one split second of excitement over recognizing something she had read about, she managed to ruin a susceptible girl's peace of mind. If this kept up, the prophecy might even be self-fulfilling.

Later, as she lay in bed hearing unfamiliar sounds, and with an unfamiliar glow of city lights tinting the room, she found her mind assaulted by some of Betty's doubts, fears, and spurious logic.

David had been with her in the car. And David was not hurt. With his Square of Protection, supposedly he was safe from danger. It was true that the truck had hit Betty's side of the taxi, but mightn't that, too, have been part of their destiny—that Betty should sit on the side of the taxi where the truck would hit?

When she thought of it that way, the whole idea seemed absurd. What would be the point of life if it were all a tightly written script in which personal effort counted for nothing?

As far as she could see, Betty had just been unlucky.

The next day Betty's neck was stiff and her head ached, but she refused to be sent home. Instead she left early in the morning for a bus tour, while others in the group set out for the secondhand bookstores.

After several hours, Mrs. Oudhousen urged them to go and see more of the city.

"Angela, this is your chance to look around. We can always order books by mail."

"Later," Angela told her. She had become absorbed. They left her alone in the store.

She had never seen so many books before, or realized how interesting they could be. It occurred to her that perhaps she could get a college education just by reading. Time

41

ticked by without her noticing, until suddenly a title leaped at her from the shelves.

She pulled it out, a large, black-covered volume on the history and practice of palmistry. It was lavishly illustrated with photographs and colored plates, old paintings and woodcuts. She wanted nothing more to do with palmistry, but the book itself was beautiful. At $14.95, it seemed a treasure.

After making the purchase, she walked back to her hotel. Betty was asleep in their room. Angela unwrapped the book and, with a stealthy glance at Betty, turned to the section on the Head Line.

There, on every point but one, Mrs. Hunt was corroborated. On that one point, the new book indicated that a steeply sloping line did not necessarily mean suicide. It could also signify an extremely morbid, depressed imagination. Betty stirred and sighed.

An extremely morbid, depressed imagination . . .

She turned the page. There, glaring up at her, was a photograph of a suicide's dead hand. She closed the book and buried it at the bottom of her suitcase.

For the next two days they toured the city. On Sunday evening they returned to Burley's Falls. As their bus pulled in at Sal's Service Station, Ross came out to meet them. His handsome face was marred by a bruised cheek and swollen lip. Spatters of reddish brown had dried on the front of his shirt.

He watched with interest as David helped Betty down the steps from the bus. "What happened to you?" he asked.

Betty smiled wanly. "I got hit by a truck."

"You go to New York and you come home like that? It must be some hell of a place."

"You don't look too good yourself," Betty retorted. "You could at least clean the blood off your shirt."

Ross looked down at the stains. "It's not mine. Some guy let his nose bleed all over me."

David was annoyed by the casual attitude. "You'd better watch yourself, man. You could land in big trouble with that lousy temper."

But Ross was on to more interesting news. "You guys heard what happened? Fabian died. The old man."

"*What?*" exclaimed Mrs. Oudhousen. "Oh, no!"

"Heart, or something," he added.

Mrs. Oudhousen wailed, "Oh, this is really shocking. We'll name the reading room after him, of course. The Anthony Fabian Memorial Library."

That night, still wound up from the trip, Angela had fitful dreams of Ross, and blood, and old Mr. Fabian. And Betty. She saw blood on Ross's hand and shirt. It reminded her of something, but she did not know what.

The next morning she entered a hushed office. In undertones, the employees speculated on what changes might take place. Leadership of the company passed smoothly into the hands of all three brothers, Mike, Bruno, and Whitman. Angela would remain Mike's secretary.

In the middle of the day, Glen came over to her desk.

"Well, Angela, it looks as if you got at least one of your predictions right."

"Do you mean about Betty Meeker?" In a village the size of Burley's Falls, everyone must have learned of Betty's accident.

"No, dear, about me." He grinned sheepishly. "I know it's crass to bring it up, but in your fortune-telling days, you said something about my inheriting money."

"Oh—yes." She was surprised that he even remembered it. "Glen, I'm really sorry. We were so shocked."

"So were we," Glen replied. "But it's to be expected. Sometime, anyway. At least he had a good life. I shouldn't

43

have said that about the money, but it just struck me that you'd mentioned it. At least there'll be enough to take you out to dinner sometime." He patted her hand and disappeared into his own office.

Two months after the trip to New York, David Bennett resigned from his job and left town. He did not tell anyone where he was going. Just out of Burley's Falls was all he said.

Betty knew no more than anyone else. When Angela visited the Meeker home one Saturday morning, she found her friend on the floor, pinning a dress pattern. Piles of fabric and paper patterns lay scattered around her.

"Hi. I'm just making a few things." Betty seemed flushed and nervous.

"What for? Are you going somewhere?"

"As far as I know," Betty said, "you're supposed to wear clothes even if you don't go anywhere."

"But so many all at once. What are you doing, getting married? Is David coming back?"

Betty readjusted a pin. "Maybe it's not David."

"Who then? Not Tom!"

"Maybe I don't have anybody in mind, but it doesn't hurt to be ready."

Angela wondered again the next day, when Tom invited her to accompany Betty and himself to the lake at Mile Gorge Park.

The park was two miles beyond their house, above the mountain road and on the edge of the Catskill escarpment. The picnic area commanded a panorama of the valley below, with the Hudson River winding through it like a tiny, shining brook. Mile Gorge Park had been named after a deep cut made by the Cat River as it tumbled and wound its way from the northern Catskills, past Burley's Falls, down into the valley to meet the Hudson.

It was a hot, humid Sunday and the park was crowded with summer visitors and local residents. Seeing no available picnic tables, they camped on the grass near the lake's edge.

They were eating lunch when Betty remarked, "David said it was the fortune you told him that made him decide to leave his job."

Angela moaned. "Oh, the idiot. It's ridiculous, the way people keep bringing that up. And you, too, Betty. Remember New York? I wish you'd all just forget the whole thing."

"What happened in New York?" asked Tom, and for the first time, learned of Betty's reaction to her accident.

Betty said defensively, "It just seemed to fit. And that scared me."

"You can make anything fit, if you try hard enough," Tom replied. He took her hand. "Where does it say that?"

"I don't—" She looked at Angela, who found the mark.

"A break in the Head Line," Angela said. "It's supposed to foreshadow an injury to the head or neck. But really, Betty, it doesn't make sense that your hand would know a thing like that before it happens."

"It depends," Betty answered, "on whether or not you believe in destiny. I guess I do, if it's nice. Angela told me I have a nice Heart Line."

"Yes," said Angela, "Betty should be getting married soon. To somebody who loves her very much."

She stared down at her own ringless finger. When they were not looking, she turned over her hand and examined the Heart Line. Was it almost as good as Betty's? She could not remember what was so good about Betty's.

They left the park early, so that Betty could go to work. As soon as she was home, Angela turned once more to the

45

book she had bought in New York. It wouldn't hurt, she thought, just to check.

Her Heart Line promised a warm and loving relationship. For the first time, she noticed an island in the middle of the line. The book gave two interpretations. According to one, it meant a guilty love affair. To the other, a time of troubles and anxiety. And who did not, at one time or another, have troubles and anxiety?

There was a cross on the Mount of Jupiter, presumably forecasting a marriage or liaison that would be materially advantageous. Another reference to the elusive marriage promised by her Heart Line. Or perhaps to the guilty love affair.

And then, in her book, she saw it—the thing that had bothered her when she dreamed of Ross's blood-spattered shirt. Someone—was it David?—said that temper of his would get him into trouble. And there it was. She had seen it in his hand on the night of the dance, but had since forgotten. Now, in her mind, she saw it again clearly, the Fate Line ending in a cross. A violent and bad end.

The Sign of the Scaffold.

6

The Sign of the Scaffold.

It was ridiculous. Destiny, again. It could not be forecast in a hand.

But perhaps it could, if a palm was able to tell anything about its owner. This was not a forecast, but a diagnosis. In Ross's case, everything about his hands pointed to something violent and uncontrollable, and Ross's temper was a fact.

He would probably laugh at her. He had every right, but she couldn't let it go. Why take a chance?

It was midafternoon. He would be leaving work soon. At the moment, the service station was quiet. She crossed the road and found him in the office, reading a book.

He looked up, frowning. "What's the great occasion?"

"You always have a chip on your shoulder, don't you?" she said. "There's no great occasion about walking over here from my house."

"You haven't done it in almost a year."

"So? Today I had nothing better to do." She straightened a girlie calender on the wall. His eyes followed her warily.

"Actually," she said, "I have a reason. Remember that time when I was palm reading?"

"When was that?"

47

"Oh, Ross. At the carnival last fall." Of course he knew. "I had some unfinished business on yours. I just remembered because I found it in a book."

"So what's the problem? You want to read my hand again? Okay, if it makes you happy." He pulled over a chair and removed a grease-smudged catalog from the desk, uncovering a recent edition of the *Kaaterskill Week*.

"Did you see the paper?" Turning to the social news, he pointed to a smiling photograph of Marcia Wollsey. She was announcing her engagement to Glen Fabian.

"So it's official now," said Angela. Quickly she skimmed the article. No date had been set. Probably they had to wait a decent interval after old Mr. Fabian's death.

She closed the paper and reached for his hand.

"Remember I said you had a temper? I can see it in your thumbs. Sometimes you have trouble controlling your temper."

He gave a contemptuous chuckle. "You really needed a book to tell you that."

"Skip the sarcasm, Ross, this just might be important. I never believed in it myself, but a lot of people seem to, so just to be on the safe side. . . . You see that little mark? That X?" She pointed to the cross on the Mount of Saturn, at the end of his Fate Line. "According to the book, that could mean very serious trouble for you, if you lose control of yourself. It could even be, well, lethal."

"So are a lot of things," he replied.

"I know it sounds stupid. But there's just enough in this, about people's personalities and certain things happening, that I think it's worth considering."

"What are you talking about? You mean you predicted something and it happened?"

"Well, you could interpret it that way, if—"

They both started at the sound of rapidly approaching

footsteps. Zinnia appeared in the doorway, her eyes narrowing at the sight of the two together.

"Well! We're getting pretty cozy around here, aren't we?"

"Just another fortune-telling session," Angela explained, "based on new research. Want me to do yours?"

"You already did. You said I'm passionate." Zinnia leaned on the door frame, exchanging a long look with Ross. Angela murmured good-bye, and left.

That night Tom went out, announcing that he was going to pick up Betty at work. It was nearly eleven when he returned, bringing her with him. Angela and her mother were on their way to bed. Florence Dawn had started to put her hair up in rollers, but quickly removed them, sensing the importance of the occasion.

While Betty sat demurely in a corner of the sofa, Tom announced that they planned to be married in the fall.

Florence clapped her hand to her mouth and started to cry. "This is the nicest thing that ever happened to me!"

Angela said, "Betty, why didn't you tell me? I asked."

"Because I wasn't—we weren't—we just wanted to be sure."

The date was set for early September. Tom had saved enough money to buy a small house, and to take a honeymoon trip to Bermuda.

"Bermuda," Betty sighed as Angela pinned the hem of her wedding dress. "I've never been to any place like that. It's so romantic, Angela."

"Are you sure you won't get homesick?"

"Not as long as I'm with Tom."

They were married on Labor Day weekend. After the reception, which was held on the lawn at the Meeker home, they boarded a New York bus to leave the next day for

Bermuda. Florence and Angela returned to an emptier house, and for a day, at least, Florence refrained from asking when the next wedding would be.

Angela had never taken seriously Glen's suggestion of a dinner date, made almost half a year ago. She did not even remember it, until the week after Tom's wedding, when she worked late one night to finish typing and organizing a lengthy project report. She was barely aware that nearly everyone had gone. Only one lit cubicle remained near the end of the corridor. Finally that light, too, went out, and Glen appeared, briefcase in hand.

"Angela, what are you doing here?"

He had known perfectly well that she was there.

"Working," she replied. "And now I'm finished."

"How about a ride home?"

"Oh, thanks, I have my brother's car."

"Your brother's car," he said, "will be perfectly safe here overnight. I thought we might stop along the way for a bite to eat. Unless you have other arrangements."

"It sounds fun," she answered cautiously, "if you can explain how I'm supposed to get back here in the morning without my brother's car, and if you can convince me that your fiancée won't mind."

As soon as she said it, she was embarrassed. Of course a dinner was nothing more than an employer's reward for a job well done.

"You ought to know," he told her, "that if I drive you home, depriving you of your usual means of transportation, I'll be happy to reverse the procedure in the morning and bring you back here. As for my fiancée, I wasn't suggesting that we elope. It was only dinner. And what she thinks is her problem, not yours."

Angela's purse and sweater lay on her desk. He slipped

the sweater over her shoulders, handed her the purse, and they left the building together.

The sun had dropped behind the mountains, leaving an amber twilight. It was a soft, warm evening, but she felt awkward and uneasy as she climbed into Glen's car and saw Tom's little Chevrolet sitting alone in the middle of the parking lot.

Glen made her relax with his easy conversation as they drove over the mountain, through Burley's Falls, past Angela's house, to La Suisse Restaurant.

God, she thought, Betty works here. And then remembered that Betty was in Bermuda.

The restaurant was built like a chalet against the hillside, surrounded by petunia beds in the summer and chrysanthemums in the fall. It was the last building in the village before the road began its winding course down the steep side of the mountain.

They were seated at a table by the window. Glen ordered drinks, a frozen daiquiri for her and a Scotch on the rocks for himself.

"Cheers," he said when the drinks arrived.

"Cheers to you." She raised her glass. "And all good wishes. When's the big day going to be?"

"Big day?"

"Your wedding."

"Oh, right. Sometime in the winter, probably." He lit a cigarette and lapsed into silence. She felt ill at ease, but could not think of anything to say.

He crushed out his cigarette. "Well, Angela, how do you like the new setup?"

"In the office, you mean? I think it's working well, but I miss your grandfather."

"Do you really? You didn't think he was sort of a martinet?"

She did not know what a martinet was. It sounded like

51

a bird. Or a European title. "I thought he was a really fine person."

"Did you? And a fine administrator? I don't know, I'd like to see someone at the top with a lot more vision than anybody's shown so far."

"How do you mean?"

"Of course it takes guts," he went on, "because you have to be ready to put security on the line in order to get something better. You've got to take chances. But we'll make it yet. Am I right?"

"You've always made it before."

"I'm talking about the future. That's your department."

"Not really. You don't believe in that, do you?"

"No, but I'm sure it can have a psychological effect."

"Oh, can it ever!"

"In a case like mine, if I were to believe what you told me, I could just forge ahead without any qualms."

"*If* you were to believe what I told you."

"That's the catch. And by the way, what did you tell me?"

"A lot of things." How could she have expected him to remember? It was only to make conversation that he brought it up now. "You have two stars. I couldn't forget that, because it's so unusual. And your Jupiter finger is long."

"Meaning?"

"Ambition. The ability to succeed."

"Well, why be theoretical about it? Here's my hand right here."

She looked down at the outspread palm and saw it all again, the long, slightly bent Jupiter finger, the high mount beneath it, the Sun Line and the two stars, the small break in the Heart Line.

But there was something else, something Mrs. Hunt had not mentioned, but which was covered in her new book. That was the fingerprints themselves. A whorled print on every finger— She could not remember what all of it meant. Some, she wished she could not remember.

"You're restless," she said. "Eager for action."

"Right. That's true. But we already know things like that about me, don't we?"

"Yes, but I *am* reading your hand. It does say all that in your hand."

"Where?"

She pointed to the pads of the fingers. "Restless. Ambitious. Clever. Eager for action. Or did I say that already? And something crooked, too."

"Crooked?"

She avoided his face and concentrated on his hand. The drink was taking hold. Her brain felt fuzzy.

He asked, "What do you mean?"

"Your finger. It's a little bit crooked, isn't it?"

His hand closed on hers. "What does that mean about me?"

"Just that your finger's a little bit crooked. Honestly, Glen, I hardly know anything about it. I only did it that one time because they drafted me. If you want somebody who really knows, you should go and see my grandmother."

"What does she really know?" He released her hand.

"Well, she seems to know what she's talking about. She says things. But when you come right down to it, they're vague. You can interpret it any way you want. That's what makes people believe it, you know."

"I didn't know you had a grandmother. Does she live around here?"

"Down the mountain. Maybe you've seen it. A little shack off the road, with a lot of chickens."

"That's your grandmother?"

She nodded. "My father's mother."

Their dinner arrived, and the subject was dropped. But

a few minutes later, Glen said, "So that's your grandmother. I'll be darned. Look, it's nothing to be embarrassed about, Angela." She had not realized her embarrassment was showing. "I've only seen the place as I drove past, but it's got a look of rugged individualism. I admire that kind of independence."

They talked long into the night, and then he drove her home. He returned the next morning, as promised, to take her to work. After that, he never referred to the evening again. They remained in the same businesslike relationship as before, lightened only by Glen's occasional teasing.

Two weeks after their wedding, Tom and Betty returned from Bermuda, tanned, happy, and looking forward to settling back into the familiar life of Burley's Falls.

For Angela, nothing changed. Probably it never would, as long as she remained at home. David had gone. Ross was lost to her forever. He was now deeply involved with Zinnia Bennett.

In October, Zinnia announced that David was planning to come home soon for a visit.

Angela was eager to see him. She supposed he knew about Betty's marriage, but wondered how he would take it. She even wondered what he would be like, the new David.

And then a disruption at the office blotted David from her mind. Mike Fabian had a heart attack.

He survived the attack, but remained in the hospital, finding it difficult to let go of his responsibilities and leave everything up to the rest of the staff. Glen took on most of his father's activities. Between the double workload, and visiting his father in the hospital, he had little time for anything else.

To Marcia, who was busy with plans for their marriage,

the lack of attentiveness seemed a personal affront. Since he was scarcely ever at home, she telephoned him frequently at the office. When he cut short her calls, she drove over to visit him.

"I don't understand you!" Angela heard her wailing from behind his closed door. She could imagine Glen, inflated with self-importance, brushing off his fiancée as though she were a fly. A few minutes later, Marcia stalked out of his office and down the corridor, her face set.

That evening, when Tom and Angela drove back to Burley's Falls, they found Marcia at Tom's house, having a glass of sherry with Betty.

Tom paused in the doorway. He had always been shy of Marcia, who seemed to him a princess.

Betty said, "Hi, hon. Look who's here."

Marcia's home and the Meekers' were not far from each other. The two girls had grown up friends, in spite of the fact that Marcia was three years older and had eventually gone away to school. After being rebuffed by Glen that day, Marcia had turned to Betty for companionship.

Betty poured sherry for Tom and Angela, and offered Marcia a refill, which she took. Already her eyes had a glassy look.

As Tom sat down, Betty bubbled, "David's back, did you know? I saw him this afternoon. Marcia and I were thinking we ought to get everybody together, maybe Sunday, and have a cookout at the park. What do you say, Tom? Angela?"

"Sounds okay," said Tom.

"Sounds lovely," said Angela. It would be a good chance to see David.

Sunday was a crisp day, but mild enough for the outdoor plans. The air was clear, the trees brilliant, and the view from the park reached well into Massachusetts. Next to the picnic ground was the lake, man-made and fed by springs. A few boats glided over its smooth, still surface.

To Marcia's annoyance, Glen had refused to come on the outing. He was spending the day at the office, catching up on his work. But David was there, and Zinnia, and a few old friends from Kaaterskill. Ross Giordano, taking a rare day off from his job, arrived unexpectedly in a lovingly renovated old Porsche.

David was almost a celebrity as he circulated, greeting everyone and telling of his adventures in Alaska, where he had learned to fly.

"You were right," he confided cheerfully to Angela. "That was no life for me, in that office."

"Oh, David!" she exclaimed in annoyance. So it really was because of her prediction. Would they never forget?

But she herself had been stupid, rushing to warn Ross about his Sign of the Scaffold.

After the lunch had been eaten and the last marshmallow toasted, Tom amused himself by burning the paper plates. Ross and Zinnia lay sprawled together on the grass. One of the Kaaterskill men produced a ball and bat.

David jumped up. "Good idea!" They began tossing the ball back and forth. Soon the other men joined them and they organized a game. Tom left his fire, and Ross managed to leave Zinnia.

Marcia gave Betty a nudge. "Do you really want to watch a ball game? They didn't invite us to play. Why don't we take a walk instead?"

Betty seemed almost embarrassed about refusing. "I think Tom would like it if I stayed here."

"Oh, you newlyweds," Marcia teased. "Angela, want to go for a walk?"

Angela would have preferred to stay and watch David

and Ross and the other men play ball, but she could scarcely admit it. She slid off the picnic table on which she sat and went with Marcia.

They headed into the woods, where the Cat River cut through the mountain and began its downward tumble into the valley. Eons of rushing water had carved a deep, wide ravine into the rock. The river now ran so far below them that they could not hear it. It was this ravine that had been named Mile Gorge.

"Is it really a mile deep?" Marcia asked as they walked along the wooded path above it.

"Not really. How could it be?" Angela replied. "They just call it that because it looks so far down. But it's deep enough."

She remembered the times when she and Tom, as children, had thrown rocks over the edge. They would count the seconds before the rocks hit the ground far below. Often they could not even hear them fall.

Marcia sighed. "I wish Glen could have come. Isn't it too bad?"

"He really is very busy," Angela said. "He's doing all his father's work and his own, too."

Marcia looked back at her with a wry smile. "Just like him. There isn't any reason why those two uncles can't share some of the load. They're all in it together."

"They are sharing, but you see, they each have their own projects. And Glen feels it's sort of a personal challenge. He has a lot of drive."

"I think he overdoes it." Marcia walked ahead, trim in her gray slacks. Specks of sunlight shone through the red autumn leaves onto her hair.

The path swerved to the very edge of the ravine. There they could look down into the gorge and see the tops of full-grown hemlocks. The sight made Angela sick. She turned away and kept to the far side of the path.

Marcia began, "Wouldn't it be nice if there was a water-fall—"

Her voice broke off in a scream. It rose shrilly above the sound of tumbling earth and rocks. Angela stood dazed, not believing.

Below her, the hemlocks reeled. At the edge of the ravine was Marcia's distorted face, her hands clinging to the root of a tree.

The root was tearing. Angela flung herself to the ground, braced her body around a tree trunk and seized Marcia's hands.

The weight was heavy, unyielding. She felt her throat ripped with screams. Saw her own screaming mouth reflected in Marcia's, the face twisted with horror.

"I'm falling!" Marcia's voice was hoarse and terrible. "Help! Help me!"

Angela's arms burned with the strain. "I—can't."

Her hold on the tree trunk slipped. Again she screamed. She was sliding—sliding toward the edge.

"Marcia, I can't! You're pulling me down. Let—go—"

Marcia's nails dug into her wrists.

"*Let go!*" Angela cried.

Again she slipped. Closer. Closer to the hemlocks in the gorge. And Marcia's face, screaming.

Earth and pebbles showered around her. Under the weight of their bodies, more ground broke away. Frantically she twisted, trying to wrench herself from the death grip. The exertion dragged her forward. Closer.

Suddenly her hands pulled free. She flung herself back. Above her she saw the trees, and the sky, dancing crazily. In her mind, she heard shrieks. Then a roaring blackness.

She crawled away from the path, through scratchy brush. Far off, she heard them calling. Too late.

The first to reach her was Tom. He dropped beside her. She buried her face against his chest.

"Oh, Tom. I couldn't hold her."

Voices asked, "What happened?" They stood around her, a ring of drained faces. "What happened?" But they knew. She heard someone say, "Who was it? Marcia?"

David and Ross inspected the path. "It broke off here, see?" David announced. "The ground gave way. Just crumbled away, right here."

And Ross muttered, "Goddam."

David said, "They should have put in a fence, or run the path up higher."

Zinnia began to sob. Tom murmured, "Angela, are you all right? You're not hurt?"

She heard her own voice, apart from the rest of her: "I couldn't hold her." Over and over again.

She looked at them all, at their horror and pity. They spoke in hushed voices, cursing the park. A few crept to the edge and looked over, trying to see Marcia. She was hidden by the trees.

Tom said, "I'll get Angela back to the car," and helped her to her feet.

Then they saw Betty. She stood alone, away from the others. Her arm circled a tree as though for support. She stared at them, her eyes black and dazed. And Angela remembered.

If anything happens to Marcia . . .

7

As they waited by the car, a physical reaction set in. The numbness left her and she huddled, shivering, inside her heavy sweater. Zinnia, red-eyed and weeping, although she had scarcely known Marcia, brought a blanket, but the shivering came from deep inside.

The park police were the first to arrive, followed by two state troopers. She told them what had happened.

"I tried to hold her. She slipped out of my hands."

Under the cuffs of her sweater, the skin was red and swelling, gouged by Marcia's fingernails.

I let her die. I let her fall and die.

She would have fallen anyway. If Angela had not pulled away, they both would have died. But she could still feel those hands clinging to hers. She would feel them for the rest of her life.

Finally the police told her she could go home. Tom got into his car.

Betty refused to ride with them. "I'll go with David."

"Come on, Bet," Tom said wearily.

Betty ran across the parking lot to David's car. Tom followed her, but came back alone a few minutes later.

"She's upset," he said. "Marcia was her friend."

Angela nodded. Tom drove her home and stayed with her. He phoned Betty to join them, but she would not.

"I suppose," Angela said, "people will always wonder if I could have held onto her just a little longer. But, Tom, I was that far from going over myself. I couldn't pull her up and I couldn't hold her."

"How could you? What was to keep you from going over, too?"

So he understood. She had not realized how tense she was until she felt her breath come more easily. He understood, but she never would. Perhaps she would never even forgive herself.

He went on, "Betty said something about calling on the family."

"Marcia's family? Oh, God."

"I think Betty's planning on going. You'd better just take it easy."

"But I was with her. I should. . . . Will you come, too?"

They drove through Burley's Falls and up the long driveway between the two spruce trees, past the tennis court. She saw it all from a trance, thinking of Marcia, who would never again play on that court, or walk through the door with the big brass knocker.

The door was opened by Mr. Wollsey. His face was a stony mask. His wife appeared calm, probably too shocked for tears. Marcia's younger sister, Heather, a green-eyed seventeen-year-old, offered them coffee.

"No, thank you," Angela said, as Tom stood by dumbly. "I just wanted to tell you I—how sorry we are."

"We appreciate what you did," Marcia's mother replied. Angela felt the blood leave her face. She murmured again that she was sorry, took Tom's arm, and left.

The funeral was held on Wednesday. Most of the people

61

who had been at the picnic were there. Tom and the other Fabian workers who knew her had been given time off from work in memory of Marcia.

Angela saw Glen at the front of the church, sitting with Marcia's family. His mother, Ramona, was there, too, with her arm around Heather Wollsey's shoulders.

A sudden and terrible tragedy, and for the survivors it would go on and on. She wondered if there was anything else she could have done. Warned Marcia to stay away from the edge? But Angela herself had not known the earth would crumble.

After the service, Tom invited her to go home with them. "For coffee, or something," he said.

She looked at Betty, who stood twisting a paper tissue into shreds. In a hoarse croak, Betty asked, "Why don't you come, Angela?"

As Tom took each of them by the arm and led them down the road toward his house, Betty began sobbing again.

"I just can't stand it. It's the worst thing that ever happened. She was so young. She had everything."

"Why should that protect her?" Tom demanded. "Having everything? Why should the lucky rich get all the breaks?"

Betty stopped crying and stared at him. "What are you, a Communist?"

"Just a guy who has to work for every penny." He steered them up the walk to the front door. More passionately, he added, "What if it was Angela that got killed? She doesn't have everything, so no big deal. Is that what you mean?"

Betty walked ahead of them into the house. "I never thought of that." She looked over her shoulder at Angela. "It could have been you."

"Don't say that." The idea was not a new one to Angela. "I don't know. I stayed away from the edge. Marcia walked right on it. She wasn't scared, the way I was."

Betty said, "It all fits in. She walked there because she had to." And to Tom, "Angela knows. She saw it in Marcia's hand at the dance last year. An early, violent death. She told me."

"Violent?" he asked in alarm.

"Not violent," said Angela. "A sudden, early fatality." But something knotted inside her as she remembered the hands.

"Are you crazy," Tom shouted, "going around saying things like that?"

"I didn't say it to Marcia! I didn't say a word, except to Betty."

"And it's true," Betty added. "She saw it, and it's true. And she saw that I was going to hurt my head, and I did, and she saw that I'll have a nervous breakdown and try to kill myself. And it's true. What she sees is true."

"You goddam—" Tom looked from one to the other, inarticulate with rage at both.

"Betty," Angela pleaded, "it just happened. It had nothing to do with any prediction."

But it *had* happened. And she had seen it a whole year ago. She had seen Betty's accident, too. And Betty's marriage, and her emotional distress, which was showing itself now.

And there was her own drowning sign . . .

"You're a couple of crazies, and I'm going to work." Tom slammed into the bedroom to change his clothes.

Betty asked, "How do you explain all the things that have happened?"

"I don't explain them," Angela said, "but can't you see? A prediction can mean anything. It's only after something happens that people decide that's it."

"Are you trying to tell me it didn't mean anything that Marcia's hand said she was going to die a violent, early death?"

"Sudden early fatality. It could have said that, and she

might have lived to be ninety. After all, it was *chance* that she walked on the edge of the path and the ground broke off. It wasn't inescapable fate."

Betty shook her head. "I wish I could believe that." She looked at the clock. "I should make him a sandwich before work. Come on into the kitchen with me."

Opening a package of sliced ham, she went on, "Do you know what I'd really like? I wish I was going to have a baby. That'd be a whole new. . . .But you said I'll be barren, didn't you?"

"*I* said that? Oh, Betty, will you knock it off? Anyway, you only just got married. How do you know you're not pregnant this minute?"

"Because I know I'm not. I was hoping—the first time—"

"Most people don't hit it the first time. Give yourself a chance. And stop that fortune-telling junk. I *cannot* see into the future."

Tom joined them for lunch. Afterward he drove his sister to the Fabian office, then proceeded to the construction site where he was working.

Angela was surprised to see a light shining through Glen's door. So soon after the funeral? When he heard her at her desk, he came out with a sheaf of papers.

"Hey, how are you? Dad gave me some letters that need answering. Can you take care of it? Just whistle if you have any questions."

His manner was flip, and he glowed as usual with life and energy. She could scarcely believe that only two hours earlier he had seen his fiancée buried. He could not have recovered so quickly.

She took the letters from him. "Glen, I didn't get a chance to tell you, I'm so sorry. I just don't know what to say."

64

"Why do you have to say anything?" His kindly tone unnerved her.

"I wish I could have done something."

"You did what you could." For a moment he almost smiled. "Did you really grab hold of her the way you said? How could you be sure you wouldn't go down, too?"

Her mouth opened slightly. "I—couldn't."

"You did it without thinking. And there you were, with only a toehold on the cliff. Her weight should have pulled you down. How did you do it?"

He knows, she thought. He knows. The room blurred. His face seemed to float in the light from the window.

He closed his hand over hers. "I'm sorry, Angela. I didn't mean to bring it all back. It must have been horrible for you as well as her. But tell me, did she suffer much?"

"She was scared," Angela said. "All the while I held onto her, she was scared, and so was I, but it didn't last long. I couldn't hold her long. I'm sure, when she fell, it was quick."

A faint smile. "Of course it was quick. You can't fall slowly."

Her hand, under his, jerked involuntarily.

He said, "I'm behaving very badly. I didn't mean that the way it sounds. You've been through a terrible experience. If there's anything I can do . . ."

"Nothing, thank you." There was nothing anyone could do.

At five o'clock she was only halfway through her work, and had to let Tom go home by himself. She would catch a bus later.

Glen's light burned on into the evening. They were the only two left in the office. He remained invisible in his partitioned cubicle until she pushed back her chair and went to get her coat.

"Angela?" he called. "Wait, I'll take you home."

As they walked out to the car, he asked, "Are you hungry? Maybe we can stop for a hamburger."

She was not noticeably hungry, but Glen insisted. Instead of driving toward Burley's Falls, he headed into Kaaterskill.

"Yes," he said, as though they had never finished their earlier conversation, "that would be the worst part. Fear. She must have been terrified out of her mind for those last few seconds. It was only a few seconds, wasn't it?"

Again she felt something catch and spin in her head.

"I don't know. It couldn't have been longer. It's just that when I look back on it, I don't have any sense of time."

"I hope you don't mind my talking about it. Sometimes it helps to talk."

She murmured an assent, and he continued, "Only those few seconds of sheer terror. Maybe you shouldn't have grabbed her at all. Just let her go. Then it would have been quicker."

"She was holding onto a tree root. I couldn't just let her go."

"You're a good girl, Angela. Quick thinker. I don't know how you did what you did, hanging onto a dead weight like that, especially when you couldn't get your back into it. You'd only your arms, and nothing much to brace yourself with."

She gazed out at the street lights, the neon signs, the stores closed for the night. Her hands tensed. She felt like screaming. How could he know? He described it exactly as it happened.

But of course he couldn't know. Afterward he had seen the spot where it took place. He probably imagined how it was.

He went on, "I wouldn't look at her when they brought

her back. Not even at the funeral. I didn't want to remember her that way. Can you understand?"

"Of course."

"My mother's taking it very hard. She was awfully fond of Marcia."

So that was the reason for her attachment to Heather at the funeral. She had already adopted a substitute.

He was silent for a moment. Then he said, "No, I don't think anybody could have done it, not even the strongest arms. Unless Marcia got a foothold against the cliff. She didn't, did she?"

With shattering clarity, Angela remembered that his house looked down on Mile Gorge Park. From it they could probably see the picnic area, but not the heavily wooded gorge itself. Still, might he have seen? But he had been at his office, miles away.

Maybe his mother . . . ? But what could any of them have seen? She *had* tried to save Marcia. To witness the rest, to see her actually pull herself away, they would have had to be there beside her.

She looked out of the window again. They were going to the Mountain Steak House, above Kaaterskill. But when they arrived, the parking lot was empty and most of the lights were out.

"Hell," he said, turning the car around. "I didn't know it was so late. Are you cold?"

"A little." She was shivering. He tapped the heater button. But the heat was already on and the car was perfectly warm.

"I'm very thin-blooded," she apologized weakly.

It was Marcia . . . Marcia . . . Marcia . . .

He stopped at an all-night diner nestled in a loop of the hairpin road.

"Good. Somebody's open. And if the coffee's not the greatest, at least it's hot. I've been here before."

The diner depressed her. Its floor was warped and its ceiling sagged. The once-yellow walls were mud-colored from the fumes of cooking. And the coffee, as he had warned her, was far from great.

He asked, "Sure you don't want anything to eat?"

She shook her head. The food looked scarcely better than its surroundings. Pies and pastries that had been standing all day were dried out, and crusts had formed on the dishes of chocolate pudding.

The place seemed to have a wretched soul of its own. Its very shabbiness, for some reason, reminded her of her father, of his shabby, wasted life. And then of Marcia—her young life, wasted.

Tears burned in her eyes. Tears for death, for sadness. For everything that ever went wrong.

"Angela!" Glen's arm slipped around her. "You're crying. What's the matter?"

She managed to shake her head, but could not answer and could not stop crying.

8

Mike Fabian went home to convalesce from his heart attack. Soon he began spending two or three hours a day at the office, leaving the rest of his work to be finished by others. Angela was forced to stay late many evenings and, coincidentally or not, found Glen doing the same thing.

Before long, she realized it was not a coincidence. He was always ready to leave when she was, and that made it natural that he should offer her a ride home. And since it was the dinner hour, it seemed equally natural that they should eat together.

"Are you getting tired of restaurant meals?" he asked one evening as she sat uneasily rearranging the stainless steelware on the table at the Mountain Steak House.

"No, I never do. At home we mostly have TV dinners. And canned pork and beans. Something easy. Nobody has much time to cook."

"Sounds dismal." He leaned across the table. He was almost touching her.

"Glen, do you know what really bothers me? And it should bother you, too. It's Marcia."

"Marcia bothers you?" He frowned slightly, his gray-blue eyes clouding over. "Look, Angela, I wasn't married to her. How long should I go on mourning a fiancée?"

"What do you mean *should*? Mourning isn't an obligation. Don't you feel it?"

He sat back, and she did, too. She had felt too strong a pull when he was close to her.

He said, "You think I didn't care enough about her. That's not true. I did. But she's gone. Mourning isn't going to change anything. Mourning seems a waste of time and a waste of emotion."

"You sound as if it's a ritual."

"Isn't it?"

She opened her mouth to answer. It was and it wasn't. Finally she said, "That's all right for you, if it's the way you feel, but what about other people? Everybody in Burley's Falls and Kaaterskill knew Marcia, and they knew you were going to marry her. Do they understand your point of view? What about her family?"

He lit a cigarette and smiled at her through the smoke. "Are you worried about your reputation or mine?"

"Nobody's reputation. It's just that—well, I was with her when she died, and—"

The rest of her statement hung between them. He would know what she meant.

"It's up to you, darling, if that bothers you," he said.

The "darling" ran through her like an electric shock. Did he mean it? She wanted him to mean it.

This shouldn't be happening, she thought. At the same time, she absorbed the rest of what he had said. If it bothered her, she could give him up.

When they left the Steak House, instead of following the road to Burley's Falls, Glen turned northward and headed farther into the mountains.

"Where are we going?" she asked.

"For a ride. Okay? Are you in a hurry to get home?"

70

"Not really."

He drove on into the dark night. She remembered hearing about a cabin the Fabians kept as a retreat somewhere in these hills.

He wouldn't, she thought. Not so soon after Marcia's death.

At a lookout spot, he pulled off the road. A steel barrier separated them from the steep descent below. Far off, she could see the lights of Kaaterskill. Other lights, from isolated houses, twinkled in the darkness. Ringing the horizon, the black outline of mountaintops was faintly visible against the night sky.

He switched off the headlights. "Ever been here before?"

"I've been here in the daytime," she said.

"This is the time to see it. Looks mysterious, doesn't it? But there's nothing out there any more. Even the wildcats are gone."

The wildcats, that had given the Catskills their name.

"They used to scream at night, those cats," he went on. "Did you know that the Dutch farmers in the valley were afraid to come into these mountains? They were afraid of the cats, and of the Indians who came here to hunt, and of the ghosts."

"Ghosts?"

"Yes, the ghosts. Those screams of the wildcats, and the sound of wind in the hemlocks—it made the settlers think of ghosts. Do you believe in ghosts, Angela?"

"Of course not."

But looking out at the vast darkness and hearing Glen talk of screaming mountain lions and the wind in the hemlocks, she pictured her father's ghost, restless, torn suddenly from life, walking the road where he died. And Marcia's, waiting at the gorge where she had fallen. Waiting . . .

Glen started the car again and drove up over the mountain.

71

He followed dark, winding roads until they reached a hill that overlooked a peaceful valley.

She knew the valley. She had seen it several times before. It didn't matter that she could scarcely see it now in the darkness.

He rested on the steering wheel and looked out into the night. She thought perhaps he was imagining the valley as it appeared by day, with its farms, its houses, its one small hamlet with the spired church, and through it all, the Cat River winding along a rocky course.

He asked, "Do you know this place?"

"I've been here a couple of times."

"This is where they're going to put in a reservoir."

"*Here*? In this beautiful little valley?"

He settled back, stetching out his legs.

"They have to put it where there's water, and where it isn't too much in the way. This won't be bad. There aren't very many people. When they made the Ashokan Reservoir, it covered seven villages and took them twenty-five years of litigation just to get the people out. Well, for one thing, that's a bigger reservoir."

"You've made quite a study of it, haven't you?" she said.

"It's my business to know these things. I even know about this, and not many people do yet, so don't go around talking, will you? They're putting in a dam and a tunnel to the Ashokan. My father plans to bid for the job."

"You don't mean the whole job! Really? It'd be enormous."

He laughed. "In more ways than one. That's why Mike and I want it, if we can get it. It could make us or break us."

She felt sad about the valley, and hoped it would never happen. She did not share Glen's excitement, but she could understand it. To a builder, building was life, no matter what had to give way.

He turned on the engine, backed his car away from the valley and started down the mountain toward Kaaterskill. But instead of continuing, he made a sharp left onto a dark, very secondary road.

"Where are we going?" she asked, her voice strangely muffled because she knew the answer.

"To my cabin. I don't know why I didn't think of it before. I've got a coffeemaker right there. We could have gone the other night, instead of that repulsive diner."

She was silent. Now was the time to say no. To put an end to it. If she wanted to.

"It's awfully late."

She spoke tentatively. He would not take her seriously. He must have known she was attracted to him. But love? She would have to decide. Now.

She would not be able to love him if he did not love her. He was attracted, as she was. He always had been. She knew it. But she was not Marcia.

"Glen, it's late."

In the faint light, she could see him smile.

"Too late for coffee? That's all I said. Just coffee. The rest is up to you."

It was a tender, caressing voice. Not the Glen she had always known.

But perhaps it was. Her mind flew in circles. He had not mourned. Maybe because—he hadn't felt like it. He said he missed Marcia. That he thought about her. Their families had been friends forever. He had known her as a child. Little Marcia. But maybe it was an expected sort of marriage, and he had gone along for lack of any better ideas. And maybe now . . .

It was all up to her, he said.

And that, she thought as the car crunched over gravel, is how these things happen.

9

She had never really thought of Glen as lovable. Rather, he was extremely attractive. Her feeling for him had been attraction, with perhaps a touch of passion. But now that she knew him better, she saw flashes of tenderness and humor that made her love him.

Once, when he happened to mention her better-forgotten fortune-telling session, she remembered the mark on her own hand that was supposed to indicate a guilty love affair.

It's true, she thought. It's happening, just like Betty's accident.

She could have had an affair with anyone but Glen. Or at any other time. It could have been five years from now. Anything else might have worked.

Guilty . . .

She tried to break it off. He countered, "Do you really want to, or do you only think we should?"

"I—"

"Forget it, then. This world is for the living. You're not going to help Marcia by giving up what we have together."

He thought it was only because Marcia was dead. He didn't know about Marcia's hands. She looked for scars on her wrists, but there were none.

Maybe it didn't really happen.

74

Maybe Marcia had fallen before Angela could catch her, and she had imagined the rest.

The only thing that kept her from crumpling was Glen himself. As a Fabian, he was powerful, and as Glen, he never wavered. He always seemed to know what he was doing, and it always came out right.

She felt that anyone who saw her must know about their relationship, but only one person seemed to have the slightest awareness of it. On several occasions, Zinnia Bennett passed by her desk while Glen was talking with her, or saw her come out of his office. Zinnia would give her a long, amused, and penetrating look, and Angela would shrivel.

But Zinnia was busy with her own life. And perhaps, Angela thought, it was not the idea of Glen that amused her, but a past love of Angela's. Shortly before Christmas, Zinnia announced that she was leaving the company to marry Ross Giordano. It was rumored at the office that she was pregnant.

Late in January, Mike Fabian returned to work full time. It meant a virtual end to the evenings Glen and Angela had spent with each other. He and his father were frequently in conference, or away on trips together.

She missed the evenings and missed Glen desperately. She tried to believe it was for the better that her life had gone back to normal with no one the wiser. Zinnia was out of the picture and no one else seemed to know or care. Marcia could rest in peace.

Zinnia and Ross had been married for two months when Angela stopped at Sal's garage on a Sunday afternoon to buy gas for her mother's car.

"Long time no see," Ross said tritely as he approached her window.

"I know. Isn't it silly, when we're such close neighbors?"

She got out of the car and followed him around to the pump. "Fill it up, please. How's everything going?"

She was amazed at the change she found in him. The aimless, carefree, slightly desperate Ross was gone, the Ross who had worked only to pay for fast cars and good times. Instead, he seemed to have a new sense of calm and purpose. All, she supposed, attributable to Zinnia.

As she stood talking with him, Zinnia drove up in the old Porsche.

Ross thumped its hood. "Know anybody who'd want to buy this thing? I can't afford to keep it going, even if I do the work myself."

"Oh, Ross, your beautiful car." Angela knew how much he had invested in the Porsche, and the pride he had taken in it. But if he had responsibilities now, they were as much his fault as Zinnia's.

Zinnia wore a baby-blue parka with a circle of white fuzz around her face. She looked like a doll.

"You should see me with my coat off, Angela. I'm out to here already."

So the rumors had been true.

Ross said, "You think it's a big game, like buying a toy. Wait till the kid starts yelling at night and you have to get up and feed it."

"*My* kid?" Zinnia laughed. "Not my kid. He's going to treat his old lady right. Angela, did you hear about David? He got a job in South America, flying for some prospecting company."

"Flying a *plane*?"

"Don't you remember? He got his license in Alaska. But he had to lie about his experience. He hardly had any, and it's dangerous up there in the mountains with those tricky air currents."

"He's crazy."

"Says he loves it. He's just sorry he didn't know sooner. You never can tell about people."

Angela drove home, thinking of David and Ross. It was almost as though the two had changed personalities.

She lay down on her bed, feeling queasy and unsettled. On and off for the past two weeks she had had the same feeling. Not necessarily in the morning, so it could not have been morning sickness. Or could it?

Oh, God, *no*.

The possibility both frightened and elated her. But it was not a very big possibility. And of course marriage was out of the question, no matter what.

The sickness went on day after day. As her certainty grew, her elation faded. She counted the time she had left.

About the middle of October, she thought. That was exactly when Marcia had died. A life for a life. She tried to avoid seeing any significance in the timing. It just worked out that way.

One night she had a dream. She was falling—falling from a mile-high cliff. She felt the scraping of rock as she struggled for a foothold.

Something held her up. A pair of hands. Marcia's face, contorted and terrified, looked down at her as she clung to keep Angela from slipping to her death. In the background, Angela could see the forest clearly. The entire scene was clear and real, but she screamed and screamed and did not make a sound. Screamed for Marcia to hold her—just one moment longer—hold her.

Then Marcia let go. Her hands opened as though she were tossing a ball. Angela tumbled away, and as she fell, caught a glimpse of Marcia, smiling.

She woke, her heart pounding. Even after she saw that she was safe, the pounding continued, but gradually subsided.

Recovering somewhat, she reviewed the dream. She had been the one who was falling. Marcia let go to save her own life. Could anyone blame her?

She did not know. She only knew that Marcia could blame *her*, and in a wordless flash, probably had. Whatever the justification, whatever would have happened anyway, she had wrenched her hands from Marcia's and let her die. Alone.

After a while she made herself stop thinking of the hands, and turned her mind to a more immediate problem. The baby.

She did not know what to do. She couldn't even tell Glen. It would only put a burden on him, for the obvious solution was out.

She would have to go away somewhere. And make up an excuse for everyone, including her own family. She would go away, get a job, and then try to decide whether to keep the baby or have it adopted.

She wanted to keep it. It was hers. But that might be too difficult, and she could not come back to Burley's Falls even for a visit. Never see her mother, or Tom and Betty. Or Glen.

She was still trying to decide what to do when Glen asked her to have lunch with him one day.

"We can't," she said, startled and disturbed. "How can we? Everybody'd see us."

"There you go again, worrying about everybody. Okay, if daylight bothers you, how about dinner?"

He was adamant. She could not get out of it. She wondered if he suspected anything.

When they were seated at the Mountain Steak House that evening, he said in a low voice, "Something's bothering you, isn't it. Want to talk about it?"

"Not particularly." She looked around at the nearby tables,

which were empty. "Not here and not now."

"Okay, then. Later."

She had not meant to tell him at all. She wondered why she was going along with it when, after dinner, instead of taking her home, he turned his car onto the north road.

To his cabin, she thought. Where all this started.

But it was not his cabin. He drove instead to the hill that overlooked the peaceful valley where they planned to build the dam.

"All right." He turned off the engine and rested his arm on the back of the seat, not quite touching her. "Let's talk about it."

She did not want to talk about it. She was afraid of what he would say, but he persisted.

"Well," she began, "since you're sort of my boss, I guess you deserve to know. I was planning to quit and go somewhere else, get a job . . ."

"What for?"

"Just to try living in different places."

"Not with that long face, you weren't. At least not without a good reason, and I think I know the reason."

"Marcia."

"And?"

She said nothing. He went on, "Look, Angela, I assume you want the kid, since you haven't done anything about it."

She nodded. So he had guessed.

He said, "Maybe I want the kid, too. It's mine, isn't it? How come you weren't going to tell me?"

"Because it's just impossible. You can see that, can't you?"

"I can see that it might appear impossible, but nothing really is. And don't forget, I have a half interest."

"No," she said, "you haven't. It's inside me, not you. If

I leave town, nobody will notice, except my mother."

"I have a half interest in the kid," he repeated, "and a whole interest in you. Now what are you going to do about that?"

She caught her breath at what he implied, then realized she was only daydreaming.

"What I planned to do," she said.

"I thought you cared about me."

"I do. But I—"

"But you're afraid of what people will think. Are 'people' more important than we are, Angela? More important than your own kid?"

"No, but don't you understand? I was alone with Marcia when she died. I mean—" She stopped, unable to say it. Again, there was no need. "I could come back in a few years. If anybody remembers, at least it will look as if we tried to be—"

"It will look worse. You're better off if you stay right here and face them down. I'll take care of you, and in time they'll find something else to put their empty minds on. Everything blows over sooner or later. Okay?"

She did not know that she had agreed, until his arm tightened on her shoulder and he pulled her close to him. He turned her face to his. She closed her eyes, and soon discarded all thoughts of going away and not seeing him again for months, or maybe years.

They flew to Las Vegas on a Friday night late in March, and there they were married. The swiftness of their elopement, and the glamor and luxury of their stay in the glittering city, provided some compensation for the shabby circumstances of the marriage. Still, it must have been a comedown for him, she thought. A humiliation, in fact, when he and Marcia had planned a large and elegant wedding, one that would do them proud both socially and professionally. She realized what a sacrifice he was making, and wondered if he honestly wanted her.

Her, or just the baby? She wondered if she would ever really be sure of him.

10

They stayed in Las Vegas for a week and then returned to the Fabian mansion, where they would live until their own house was built. The house he had planned for Marcia.

"Didn't get very far," he explained to Angela. "It was still being designed when she died, but we'll start it up again. Just hang on for a few months. Maybe a year."

A whole year of living at Villa Fabiani with her in-laws: his parents and bachelor uncle, Whitman, and in another house on the same estate, Bruno with his wife and daughters. Any in-laws would have been constraining, but these were intimidating. Quite possibly she was never meant to be a Fabian, especially a Fabian out of necessity.

"We shouldn't have done this," she told him as they drove back to Burley's Falls from the airport.

"No regrets," he said. "It's wasted emotion."

"Like mourning."

"Exactly. Don't worry about it, angel, they'll love you."

She doubted it. She knew how they must feel. A lump of apprehension grew inside her as they drove through the village, past La Suisse Restaurant and the community center.

Now she could see the mansion. From the road below, it looked like a glass palace, its many windows blazing with reflected rays from the setting sun. Glen turned sharply onto a narrow road flanked by a pair of concrete gateposts with crouching lions on top. The driveway was a long one, winding in S curves up the steep hillside.

And then the house, a mass of gray stone. The road looped past the front door under a carriage roof. As soon as Glen stopped the car, a middle-aged woman in a black dress appeared at the door. He greeted her cheerily.

"Stella! Meet the new Mrs. Fabian. Angela, this is Stella, our right-hand lady."

From around the corner of the house came a man wearing a red plaid jacket. He took the suitcases from the car and carried them inside. Glen introduced him as Albert, Stella's husband. Between them, they managed the Fabian estate, with help from local dayworkers.

Glen's two teenage cousins, Grace and Linette, came out next. They were Bruno Fabian's daughters, eager to meet the new bride.

"Ramona's in the living room," they volunteered, "in case you want to see her."

When Angela had removed her coat and boots, Glen led her through a dizzying series of rooms. "You could get lost in here," she whispered, hurrying to keep up.

"You'll learn your way around," he said.

The living room was almost as vast as the lobby of their Las Vegas hotel. At the far end of it, seated on an immense sofa, was his mother, Ramona, with a silver coffee service on the table in front of her, and beside her, Heather Wollsey.

"Oh!" cried Heather, wide-eyed, her hand to her mouth.

"We were just having some coffee," Glen's mother explained. "We didn't expect you back so early."

There were three empty cups. Grace and Linette had been there, and probably their mother. And Heather was abashed at having been caught lingering. Because this was a family occasion—or because Angela was Marcia's replacement? Angela, remembering the clinging hands and screaming face, could not look at her.

"The coffee's almost gone," Ramona apologized. "I'll ask Stella to bring some more."

"None for me, thanks." Glen passed a cup to Angela. While the others talked, she sipped it in silence and looked around the room.

The sofa on which Ramona sat was cherry red, and the longest she had ever seen. She wondered if it had been custom-made. Above it hung a portrait of what she assumed was the first Fabian. Other family members, on a smaller scale, were displayed in photographs on a table beside her. She recognized Glen as a child, Glen in cap and gown; his cousins Grace and Linette in various stages of growing up, skiing, horseback riding.

There was one of Glen and Marcia standing by a ski tow at Hunter Mountain. Snow was on the ground. She thought it had probably been taken a year earlier, the winter or spring before Marcia died. Only a year ago.

After a while Heather excused herself, and Glen murmured something about shaking off the dust of travel. Ramona said, "I've moved you into the east apartment, Glen. You'll find everything there."

"An apartment?" Angela asked as he led her back through the various rooms.

"That's what they call it. It's got everything except a kitchen, so we'll be taking meals with the folks."

They climbed a broad staircase, then walked down a carpeted corridor to the suite that was to be their first home.

To her, it seemed awesome and lavish—a marble fireplace in the sitting room, gracious traditional furnishings in rich burgundy and cream to pick up the tones of the Oriental rug, and two long French windows, one of which opened onto a small balcony.

"Well, here we are," he said.

She nodded, and looked out at the snowy mountains covered with a gray screen of trees.

"It's lovely."

It was strange, a home that had been handed to her all complete, instead of created by her. In addition to the spacious sitting room, there was a large corner bedroom with a king-size bed, two smaller rooms, and two bathrooms. It was nearly as big as a whole house all by itself.

Glen said, "Better start getting organized, dear. We eat at seven."

At that, she felt a pang of homesickness. "Could we ever eat up here by ourselves?"

He laughed. "Sure, if we bring it in. But why? Stella's a good cook."

"They're your family. You're used to them."

"I know how you feel. We'll have our own place eventually."

She spent the next hour unpacking, finding a skirt to wear to dinner, and settling into her new way of life. It was unquestionably luxurious. If she had to live with her in-laws for a while, this was the best way to do it. At least the apartment had privacy. Only one thing marred it for her: the windows of the living room and bedroom looked out over Mile Gorge Park.

Dinner that night was a clan affair. Besides the immediate household of Glen, herself, his parents and Whitman, Bruno and his family came to join them. That was not unusual, Angela found, and the occasion was not necessarily herself, but merely a chance for a family get-together with much conversation about the business.

After dinner the women dispersed while the men moved to one end of the table and continued their talk. Angela returned to the upstairs apartment to wait for Glen.

She waited an hour. Two hours. She grew chilly in her

fluffy peignoir, and put a sweater over it. After another hour she changed to a flannel gown and fleece robe. At every sound, she would look toward the door. The old house creaked in the wind, but the door remained closed. She fell asleep on the sofa and woke when the doorknob turned. At that moment the mantel clock struck a half hour. It was one-thirty in the morning.

She blinked up at him. "Where were you?"

"Downstairs," he replied. "Where else would I be?"

"I was waiting for you. Our first night—I thought—"

"It's hardly our first night, is it?" He sat down to take off his shoes and socks. "I'm sorry, I didn't know you were waiting. When we get wound up like that—"

"It's okay."

It wasn't, really, but she refused to argue about it. She did not want him to be sorry he had married her.

"You see, Angela, I love my work." With his arm around her, he led her into the bedroom, lay down beside her and pulled the quilted spread over them.

She laughed at the contrast between his activities and his words. "Can't you ever stop talking about business, even at a time like this?"

"That's what I'm trying to tell you. I want you to know right from the start how important it is to me, so you'll know what to expect."

"Glen, I've been working with you for four years."

"It's more than just work. It's even more than pleasure. Remember once you told me I was going to be very successful in business?"

"You already are," she assured him.

"That's not me personally. The company was there before me. But I think I have a talent for it. I guess you could sense that, couldn't you, and that's why you predicted what you did."

"Do you think so? You don't think I was more sincere than that?"

"Were you?"

"I studied a whole book. I didn't tell anybody anything that wasn't in the book."

"Has any of it come true?"

"A few things, but that was just coincidence. After all, it's possible that a hand could reflect certain things about a person's character, but it's ridiculous to think it can tell the future."

"Maybe some of the things that happen to people are inherent in their characters."

"Maybe. But not a thing like Betty getting hit by a truck, or—"

"Or what?"

She did not answer. Gently he prodded, "What else did you predict that came true?"

"Something. I didn't predict it, exactly. I just saw it, but I didn't say anything. I was too—" Again she hesitated.

"Come on, mystery woman, what's the big deal?"

"It's not a big deal. I just—"

"Something about me."

"No, not about you. It was—all right, it was Marcia."

He was silent, watching her. When he echoed "Marcia?" his voice was hoarse.

"I know it sounds crazy, but there was a break in this line, in both hands. My book said a 'sudden, early fatality.' "

"When did you see that?"

"In her hand? At the carnival. That's the only time I ever looked at her hand."

"Angela—"

"I know it sounds crazy, but that's the truth. Of course I didn't tell her. How could I tell her?"

"You saw it at the carnival? Really?"

87

"Yes. I know what you're thinking. A whole year before it happened."

"Did you mention it to anybody?"

"Only Betty Meeker. My sister-in-law. She—after Marcia died, she was furious with me. As if my predicting it made it happen."

Again, silence. Then he said, "Tell me again how you saw that in her hand."

"It was here." She showed him her own hand. "The Head Line. There was a little break in it under the second finger. That's the Saturn finger. She had it on both hands."

"When you saw it—" He stopped, as though unsure how to phrase what he wanted to know.

"It scared me," she said, "except that I just didn't believe it."

"Do you believe it now?"

"No, not really. I think Betty does, my sister-in-law. But it was just chance.. Marcia wanted to go for a walk because the guys were playing ball. And she missed you. If you'd been there, or we were all playing—or something—or if she wasn't curious about the gorge, so that she walked near the edge to see it—"

"You don't think she would have got it another way? Another time?"

Angela was brought up short. The possibility had never occurred to her.

"Glen, you don't believe that."

"I don't know what I believe, but that's what the fatalists would say."

"It's just not logical."

"Dear, logic is keeping an open mind. Think of all the people who used to insist the earth was flat. Anybody could see it was flat. And if you disputed that, you were some kind of nut."

88

"That's different."

"It's not the least bit different." He turned on the lamp above the bed. "Come on, let's see what else is here. It might be something that needs immediate action."

"I've already done this twice," she protested.

"So do it a third time. What's wrong with that?"

She did not want to do it a third time. She could not stop thinking about Marcia, but he held his hand up to the light and waited for her to begin.

She scarcely needed to look at it. "It's all still there, your head ruling your heart. And I guess that's true. You're the one who thinks mourning is a waste of effort."

He said nothing. She went on, "Ambition, success. It's still the same. I don't know why you want to hear it again. And this index finger of yours, the finger of Jupiter."

"What about it?"

"I told you, remember? That's the key to you. That's your ambition, and the ability to succeed."

"Why, because it's crooked?"

"No, silly, because it's long. That's the ambition part."

She remembered telling him it was crooked. Or slightly bent. It was the night they had dinner at La Suisse, and perhaps she mentioned it only because of the drink.

A bent finger was supposed to mean that success would be achieved by devious means. But maybe it did not necessarily mean bad devious means. Or maybe a truly crooked finger was much more bent than Glen's, which had only a slight angle to it.

"Come on," he said. "You told me all this before."

"That's what I said. There's really nothing new." She turned his palm to look at the edge. "One marriage. Two children."

"Two!"

"Be glad it's not two dozen. Oh, wait!"

"What?"

Without thinking, she had pounced on the thing that had puzzled her the first time she saw it, the break in his Heart Line under the Mount of Saturn.

"Well, what?" he asked again.

"This." She touched it lightly. "This little break. When I saw it before, at the Halloween dance, I didn't know what it meant. I thought it might be heart trouble, but my new book says it's a loss of love through fatality. Glen, that could be Marcia."

"What the hell are you talking about?"

Because she had mentioned Marcia again?

"I just—well, that's what the book says. But you weren't even engaged to her when I saw that."

He sat up, held his hand directly under the light, and studied it closely.

"I'll tell you, Angela, if what you're saying is true, maybe there really is something in this."

"There can't be. It was an accident, what happened to Marcia. It just *happened*. I still don't believe—"

"That it's preordained? Kind of farfetched, even though there are people who would differ with you on that. But the rest of it— There's no reason to think the rest of it isn't true. The possibility of things to come. That it's all set up. All there for the taking, if you'll take it."

He switched off the lamp. "Just like something else I don't need to mention."

In the dark she felt his face very close to hers, his fingers groping at the buttons on her nightgown.

11

A few days after their arrival at Villa Fabiani, Glen bought her a car, a yellow compact. The next morning she drove to her mother's house to pick up some of her possessions. Florence was dressing for work, struggling into a too-tight skirt.

"They're saying things about you," she told her daughter, as she glared at her reflection in the dressing-table mirror.

"What sort of things?" They had eloped as quietly as they could, hoping to make their marriage a fait accompli, with no public announcement and no identifiable date.

"About you marrying him. How'd you expect to keep that a secret? And I even heard—"

"What?"

Angela did not need to ask.

"I heard them talking about Marcia. About when she fell that time."

"Oh, God." Inevitable though it might have been, it still came as a shock. "Did they say anything about me?"

"No, they knew I was listening. And the people around here always liked you, but—"

"Yes, I know. I know what it could look like." She only wondered if they had put it into words.

"It would have been better if you didn't marry him," Florence said.

"You know why I had to. And I do love him."

"Well, then, I guess you gotta take your lumps. But if you ask me. . . . Actually, they're talking more about him. About why he went and got married so soon after she died. If people say things about you, maybe it's because they're a little bit jealous. You'll just have to put up with that."

Angela put up with it and more. She tried to behave naturally, as though nothing had changed, whenever she met any of the townspeople. After a while, some of the chill began to thaw. But there would probably be questions, at least in their minds, for a long time to come.

The weeks plodded by. They would stretch into months before the baby was born. She, who had always worked and thought it would be fun to loaf, now felt the deadliness of it. And she saw less of Glen than she had before she married him. With no more need to court her, he worked late into the evenings, and often on weekends. When he did come home, he would spend hours downstairs, as he had on the first night. But she was growing used to it, and would simply go to bed without him.

One night in May she woke to a commotion of voices and hurrying feet. She threw on a bathrobe and went out to the hall. Downstairs, two members of the volunteer emergency squad were bringing in a stretcher. Glen's father had had another heart attack.

Glen met the ambulance at the hospital. Once again he began a heavy schedule of commuting between the office and Mike's bedside. After a day and a half he returned home, haggard and exhausted, to report that his father was out of danger.

Angela asked, "What about you? Are you trying to get

sick, too? Why don't you let your uncles take care of the office?"

"Because the office is where Mike needs me." He ran a hand over the stubble on his face. "Do you know what happened the last time he was out? No, you don't. There was a job he wanted very badly. Never mind what it was. Those guys didn't have the nerve to bid for it. I found out just before the deadline."

"How come I didn't know about that?" she demanded. "I was working for Mike. What job are you talking about?"

"I said never mind what job. A lot of things happen before they ever get down on paper, so you wouldn't necessarily know. The point I'm trying to make is, you can't go at this stuff half-assed, and that's what those two are trying to do. If I leave it up to them, we'll be out of business in a month."

"Was it the dam?"

"No, it wasn't. They haven't asked for bids on that yet. It takes a long time." He went into the bedroom, lay down, and instantly fell asleep.

Mike Fabian remained in the hospital, neither improving nor growing worse. Every few days, Angela paid him a visit. She had always felt a certain fondness for Mike. It distressed her to see him laid low.

In June, Zinnia's baby was born. After a brief chat with her father-in-law, Angela went to the maternity floor. She found Zinnia sitting up in bed, wearing a lacy pink night-gown.

"Did you see the baby?" Zinnia asked. "She's near the window in the nursery. It says 'Girl Giordano, seven pounds, one ounce,' and she's gorgeous. Come on, I'll show you."

She really was pretty, Angela thought as they stood in front of the nursery window. Very pretty for a newborn.

93

Her face was already well filled out, and her hair was thick and black. She had a dainty mouth and large dreamy blue eyes, which Zinnia was sure would darken.

"Isn't it fun? I'm a mother," Zinnia bubbled when they returned to the room. "And she's so beautiful. I think Ross wanted a boy, but I was holding out for a girl, and I got it."

"How is Ross?"

"He's okay." Zinnia sat back on the bed, her face drawn in sullen lines. "I don't know. He says he's sick of pumping gas. Honestly, I don't know what that man wants. I think—" She gulped and looked pathetic. "I think he wishes he wasn't stuck with the baby and me. Then he could try something better."

"He said that?"

"Not exactly, but I know what he thinks. And it's silly. Anything you do all day is boring. Does he think I'm going to have such a great time changing diapers?"

"I can hardly wait to change diapers, myself," Angela said with a smile. "I'm so bored. What are you naming the baby?"

"Katie June. That was my idea. If it was a boy, we were going to name it after Ross."

Katie June was less than a month old when her father had a falling out with Sal and left his job.

"He quit?" exclaimed Angela when Betty told her about it. "With a wife and baby? What are they going to do?"

"I don't know if he quit or if it was mutual," Betty said. They were drinking iced coffee on the patio Tom had built one weekend in back of his house. "I guess he'll just have to find something else, but this is a bad time. Angela, couldn't he work for Fabian?"

"Why not? Why doesn't he just apply?"

The more she thought about it, the less she could imagine

Ross "just applying" to a firm that was partially owned by his ex-girlfriend's husband. But if a job were offered to him . . .

The next morning Glen woke her to make love. For that, she did not mind being waked. Afterward she lay in their bed watching him dress, while a summer breeze blew through the open window.

"You know Ross Giordano?" she asked. "He used to work at Sal's. He's a really good mechanic, and I heard he's looking for a job. You wouldn't happen to have anything at Fabian . . .?"

Glen paused in the middle of reaching for a tie from his extensive collection. "Giordano. You had some kind of attachment there once, didn't you?"

"Ages ago. Yes, I dated him a few times. After all, we went through school together, all the way from kindergarten."

"And what is your particular interest in this?"

"No particular interest. I just thought—you're the biggest employer around here. And his wife used to work in the office. Zinnia Bennett. Remember?"

"Ah, yes, Zinnia. Now tell me, what can this boyfriend of yours do? Most of our jobs are skilled, you know."

"I just told you, he's a topflight mechanic. He can fix anything. It's just that he and Sal—"

"Where'd he learn?"

"I don't know. He was born that way."

"It's not enough."

"How do people get skilled, anyway?" she demanded. "When Tom started, he was just out of high school with nothing but a driver's license, and they taught him how to handle the truck. Are those skills so hard to learn?"

"We don't need truck drivers at the moment, and we don't need mechanics."

She doubted that Glen really knew what they needed. He had very little to do with grass-roots hiring, but he could have put in a word.

"I'm only asking for a friend," she said. "I told you, I've known Ross all my life. In third grade—" She raised her voice as he went into the bathroom. "In third grade, I couldn't bat the ball, so he did it for me and let me run to first base."

"We don't need batters, either."

"The other kids laughed at me, but—"

"You played baseball in third grade? Isn't that a little rough?"

"Softball. Glen, he has a wife and baby."

"So of course the world owes him a living. Well, I'll tell you, I might consider hiring his wife. Some of the guys have missed her down at the office."

Before the week was over, he had done exactly that. Zinnia took the job eagerly, not only for the money, but for something to do. Angela remembered Ross's comment about the baby being a new toy. Now that she had had it for a while, Zinnia was ready for some other amusement.

In summer, the building season was at its height, and Mike Fabian was still in the hospital. With Glen away so much of the time, Angela was more bored than ever. She had grown tired of television, tired of reading and listening to music, and even of taking walks in the woods. For a while she had enjoyed making plans for the new house, but then, to her dismay, found that work on it had stopped. Temporarily, Glen said. The men had been transferred to more urgent commercial projects, leaving nothing but a hole in the ground. She had the feeling that Glen did not really care.

In the middle of summer his hours grew even later: eleven, twelve, one o'clock. She thought it might have something to do with the proposed dam. They could be planning their cost analyses for the bid. Maybe. She often woke during the night, and then watched the clock until he came in.

One Friday she went to bed very early. The day had been hot and it scarcely cooled off at night. She turned on the air conditioner, but still could not sleep. Midnight passed. One o'clock. Then it was nearly two. She telephoned his office. No one answered. She turned on the radio, listening for disaster reports. After a while she got up and went out to the balcony off the living room.

Below her was Burley's Falls. She could see only one light shining through the trees, and wondered whose it was.

To her left was the deep darkness of Mile Gorge. She shuddered, thinking of Marcia. The gorge would never again be a mere ravine. It would always be imbued with Marcia's presence. She shuddered again and hurried inside.

Finally, through the window, she saw the lights of a car moving swiftly up the hill. A few minutes later, Glen came into the suite. He paused in the doorway, startled to see her awake.

She said, "I was afraid you had an accident." Then she smelled his breath. "Some accident."

He grinned. "Just a little lubrication. When you're working half the night, you need something to keep the machinery oiled." He walked past her, removing his loosely hanging tie.

"You were working?" she asked. "Where? I called your office a while ago."

"What'd you do that for? Did something happen?"

"I was worried about you, believe it or not." She followed him into the bedroom. "Glen, do you really care about me?"

"What brought that on?" he asked.

"Because—you never used to work this late when Marcia was alive, even after your father got sick."

He put his finger under her chin. A tender gesture, but

his voice was cold. "Now you just take it easy, angel. I don't want to hear another word about Marcia. It doesn't become you. Understand?"

She understood. She watched him untie his shoes and go into the bathroom. After a while she heard the shower running. It ran for a long time. He did not want to come out to her. He did not want to talk or come home to her. And he wouldn't even take off his clothes in her presence. Only his shoes.

Was it Zinnia? she wondered.

She thought it possible, and even more so a few days later when she went to the new library to return a book. Ross was at one of the tables, reading. He looked up, saw her, and went back to his book.

On her way to the fiction shelves, she passed his table. "Hi, Ross, how's it going? How's the baby, and Zinnia?"

She caught the words *Construction Engineering* before he rested his elbows on the book.

"She's okay," he said.

"Zinnia or the baby?"

"The baby. I don't see much of Zinnia. She works a lot of overtime."

Angela felt a flush creep over her face. His eyes narrowed. She said lamely, "Yes, summer's a busy time. And with Mike in the hospital—"

Ross closed his book, returned it to its shelf, and left the library.

The summer wore on, with days spent by the swimming pool in back of the house, or in her air-conditioned rooms. Life was more social now, as Bruno's wife, Fay, and her two daughters spent much of their time by the pool. The girls usually had their teenage friends and house guests clustered about them, and the two older women had each other. Angela hung on the fringes, feeling a part of neither group.

One day in early August, as the three Fabian wives were eating lunch by the pool, a telephone rang inside the house. Stella came to the door. "For you, ma'am."

Ramona went to pick up the nearest extension. A moment later they heard her voice, shaken. "Fay, will you come here?"

Fay dropped her fork and ran into the house. Angela heard a garble of hurried words, a voice breaking emotionally. She pushed back her chair and went inside. Fay was in the process of dialing the phone.

"That was the hospital," she told Angela. "Mike just died."

"Oh, no!" In her shock, Angela could not think what to say. "Is there anything I can do?"

Fay went on with her phone call. To the office, asking for Bruno. Feeling helpless and sad, Angela crept up to her room. Exept for Glen, Mike had been her favorite member of the family.

When Bruno and Whitman arrived home an hour later, she went down to join them. The family, all but Ramona, had gathered in the library. Fay hurried toward her.

"You haven't heard from Glen? I can't understand it. Why won't he come home?"

Whitman said, "He'll be along. He thought there might be some arrangements to make at the office."

Ramona appeared in the doorway, her face stiff and ashen. She pushed past Angela into the room.

"Where is Glen? Doesn't he know?"

"Yes, of course he does," said Whitman. "He stayed at the office, in case—" He could not seem to think what it was that Glen had stayed in case of.

At six o'clock, Glen finally came home. He embraced his

mother, gently patting her back, and then started upstairs. Angela followed. As they climbed the stairs, she tried to tell him how sorry she was. He had his back to her and did not answer. But when they reached the upper hallway, he paused, his eyes glittering feverishly, and took her hand.

"This is it, angel. My turning point. I stayed in the background while he was alive because I respected the guy, but that's all over now. Do you know what I mean? Starting today, there's nothing holding us back."

She was stunned. "Glen, how can you talk like that? Don't you feel anything?"

He nodded calmly. Still numb, she decided. Grief could make a person numb. She said, "You didn't mean that, did you? What you just said. The three of you will be working together."

"Is that a habit of mine? Saying things I don't mean?"

"But it sounded as if. . . . Was it in the will?"

"Nothing's on paper, dear. We're supposed to be men of honor." When they entered their suite he walked over to the window and gazed out at the mountains, at the bright summer evening.

"But you know," he added, his eyes still on the scenery, "it's not very honorable to let a good company like Fabian be ruined through incompetence."

He could not mean his uncles. And yet that was the only thing he could have meant. Did he really believe they were incompetent? Or did he want—power?

His own uncles. His family.

His back was still to her, but as she moved closer, she could see part of his face. Something resembling a faint smile tightened the corners of his mouth. She thought: This isn't Glen. He's different.

"How is this supposed to happen?" she asked. "Are you buying them out?"

The smile broadened. "I think we'll just wait and see."

She knew his plans were already made. They were the reason he had stayed at the office that afternoon.

"I don't see how you can do that!" she exclaimed. "With your father just dead, I don't see how you can be so—"

"We're back to that again? I thought you understood my point of view. I never disputed your right to yours. I suppose your way could make a certain amount of emotional sense, but all that sentimentality isn't really going to change anything. You might as well keep moving ahead, and for me, this was the time to do it."

Catching everybody off guard. She marveled at his cool resolve in the face of loss. Marveled, but did not like it.

"That was privileged conversation, dear," he added. "You understand that, don't you?"

Of course she understood it. And perhaps she understood Glen, too, better than she had thought. This might have been his way of dealing with grief—by denying it and keeping busy. It was rather pitiful. Almost sadder than if he had given in.

He would never give in. He could not believe they expected him to, although they had been at him day after day since his father's death. "Barely cold in his grave" was the trite phrase that flashed through Glen's mind. Barely cold, and already they were trying to scuttle his ideas.

"But we aren't equipped to take on a project like that," Bruno argued, after Glen had put through a call to the Water Resource people. It was almost laughable the way Bruno had come charging into his office when he overheard part of the conversation.

Glen raised an eyebrow. "Why not?"

"I should think it's obvious. We just don't have the capacity."

"How come Mike was willing to try?"

A good argument, but it cut no ice with either of his uncles. A couple of pantywaists. As though the capacity of the company were a static thing.

He got some solace from Zinnia, who was now his secretary. She believed in him. Or so she said. Probably she said it only to please him. He had a feeling she didn't really understand what it was all about. Just as well, in some ways, but he would have preferred a more intelligent secretary. And the way things were going, he began to regret having been personally involved with her. She had started taking him too much for granted. Even making demands on him.

"I thought I was going to see you tonight," she whined, pouting coyly as she stood beside his desk.

"I've got work to do, Zin."

"That's all you ever do. You used to have time for me. What happened? Don't tell me you decided to go back to dear little wifey."

"You may have noticed, dear little secretary," he pointed out, "that I never left dear little wifey. It's true I used to have time for you and now I don't. But I'll tell you what. If you'll be patient for another hour, I'll take you to dinner."

She settled down happily, not knowing what was in store for her. He, too, was content with his plan, until later, when they were seated at La Suisse, and then he remembered.

Good God, the sister-in-law worked there.

One afternoon a few days later, Angela stopped to visit Betty on her way back from Kaaterskill where she had bought furnishings for her nursery.

She thought that, for a moment, Betty's eyes glistened enviously. Betty had almost given up on having a child of her own. And then she said, "Maybe it will make him shape up a little, when the baby's born."

"What do you mean?" asked Angela.

"Well, because—you know I'm only working lunchtimes now, but one of the girls I know who works at dinner told me she saw him there the other night. With Zinnia. Maybe I shouldn't have told you, but I thought you'd want to know."

"Yes, I would," Angela said. "Thank you. Well, after all, she's his secretary. He used to take me out, too, when I worked there."

"And look where you ended up," Betty said pointedly. "Anyway, this wasn't just—I mean—" She blushed, and Angela wondered how they had behaved with each other. In public, too. She trusted Glen's discretion, but not Zinnia's.

"Anyhow," Betty concluded, "both of you were single back then. That was different."

"Yes," agreed Angela, "it sort of was."

After dinner that night, at which she had eaten almost nothing, she lay on her bed and counted the hours before he might come home. She tried to think of what she would say to him. It was hard to concentrate. She twisted and turned, but could not find a comfortable position. A backache nagged her until finally she fell asleep.

Strange dreams floated through her mind. She saw Mile Gorge Park and the people who had been there on the day of the picnic. She saw Marcia. In her dream, she knew she had the day to live over again, and this time Marcia would not die. She felt great joy and relief. Marcia's death seemed a nightmare from which she was finally waking into reality. Now everything would turn out the way it was meant to be. Instead of Glen, she would marry David Bennett.

She woke briefly, shocked by the idea. Glen was her husband and she loved him, in spite of his quirks and grandiose ideas. She did not love David Bennett.

She sank again into restless sleep. Again and again she dreamed of her baby. She dreamed it was being born at home, her childhood home. She was there alone. Over and over again the baby was born, one swift dream after another, until she woke, feeling a cramp. It lingered for a moment, then vanished.

She stared at the ceiling. The baby *was* being born.

All around her the house was quiet. The clock said eleven-thirty. Everyone would be asleep, and Glen had not come home.

But it was too soon for the baby. It couldn't be happening. And yet it was.

She telephoned her doctor, then dressed quickly and started down the stairs. Before she reached the first floor, a pain doubled her over.

"Are you all right?"

Stella, wearing a wrapper, stood in the dining room doorway.

"The—baby," Angela gasped. Stella needed no further explanation. She hurried to wake her husband.

They reached the hospital in twenty minutes. The world became a blur of lights, voices, and pain. Then blackness. Through the blackness, a voice called to rouse her.

They told her she had a son.

12

They had planned to name the child Michael, after Glen's father. Now that he was born, Angela added the middle name Howard, for her own father.

She had been taken to her room and had fallen asleep. It was still dark when she was awakened by a disturbance in the hall. She heard Glen's voice, speaking loudly. "You can't keep me out of here. It's my wife and kid."

She watched him come through the lighted doorway and stand beside her bed. For a moment, neither of them spoke. Then she asked, "Were you having a nice time tonight? I wasn't."

He sat down on the edge of the bed. "Why the hell didn't you call me?"

"Call you where?"

"At the office. Where else?"

His face was a study in seriousness. Perhaps he really meant it. She could only say, "You wouldn't have gotten home in time. Why weren't you home?"

"Darling girl, how was I to know this was the night? You said October." As though she had done it on purpose. "If you'd called me, I would have dropped everything."

"Including Zinnia?"

He stiffened. "What about Zinnia?"

She was exhausted, but had to finish what she had started.

"You didn't really think I was stupid," she said. "You just didn't care what I thought. All those late nights. It was one thing, off in the mountains, but you, might have had the decency not to humiliate me in public."

"Public?"

"La Suisse."

"Oh, that." He grinned, suddenly and engagingly. "All we had was dinner. What did you think we'd do there?"

She wished he would leave and let her sleep. After a moment he began to laugh.

"Humiliate you? That's a slight distortion. If you want to know, I had to fire the girl. I just decided to take her out to soften the blow."

"Fire her? Why?" She hated herself for the pleasure it gave her, and for not caring, at least at the moment, about Zinnia and her future.

"She's not really very efficient." He took her hand. It was the first time he had touched her since he came into the room. "You know something? I haven't seen my son."

He left her and went to the nursery, where, as a brand new father, he was allowed to view his child even at that odd hour. She was almost asleep when he returned to inform her that Michael was a good-looking kid.

"Michael Howard," she said. "Is that all right?"

"Why Howard?"

"My father."

"I see." He did not sit down again, but wandered about the room. "Michael Howard. He's kind of early, isn't he?"

"About six weeks. But he's healthy enough. Five pounds, four ounces."

Glen stood at the window, looking out at the stars. He couldn't, she thought in sudden panic, be doubting that the baby was his. He must have realized there was nobody else. Not even a possibility, except Ross, and he had been married by then, which Glen might not have considered significant. But Ross had darker coloring. Couldn't Glen see that?

He turned from the window. "It's been a long night." It certainly had. He bent briefly to kiss her, and left.

She never knew what he had thought in those moments by the window. After that night, he seemed to revel in fatherhood. He visited her often, sometimes twice a day, and sent batches of flowers that delighted the nurses and impressed the other visitors. When she and the baby were discharged from the hospital, Glen was on hand to drive them home, even though it meant taking several precious hours off from work.

Now that her days were no longer idle, she felt her existence was justified. What was more, in Zinnia's absence, Glen's working hours miraculously shortened. He was home by six or seven every evening. They were a family again. A real family, with a child.

"You know, you had me scared for a while," she told him one night as he watched her put Michael to bed after a late feeding. "You were working all that overtime, and Zinnia was, too, and her husband knew about it. And then somebody saw you—"

"I explained about that," he reminded her.

"Yes, but I was afraid. . . . You see, I do know Zinnia. And I know what kind of guy Ross is. I was afraid he might go after you."

"Go after me? Why me? By the same token, he could have slaughtered half the county, but he didn't. You might be interested to know, your stalwart friend lost his nerve."

"Ross? What do you mean?"

"Took off. Decamped. Left town. The law might even call it desertion. Not that she wasn't asking for it."

"Whatever she was asking for, knowing Ross, it wasn't that. But I'm glad he just took off instead of attacking somebody. He doesn't need more trouble."

Ten days later, Zinnia herself left Burley's Falls to stay with a friend in Saugerties, where she thought she might have a better chance of finding a job. Ross, it was said, had gone to New York. Of their little family, only Katie June remained, in the care of her Bennett grandparents.

Within a few weeks, Glen again began to spend more time at the office. Angela wondered who it was this time, but soon deduced that it was not a woman, but the dam.

"Why does it mean so much to you?" she asked. "You're letting it run your life. There are plenty of other projects."

She had been asleep, but had gotten out of bed when she heard him come in, and then heard silence. She had found him in the living room, trying to relax with a glass of whiskey.

"Whatever I told you," he said impatiently, "wouldn't make sense, at least not to you. It means a lot to me because it's big. Can you understand that? Because of the size, the scope, the importance. It reaches out into other areas. Aside from that, we can grow as a firm. We'll be in a whole new league."

"But, Glen—"

"Never mind 'but, Glen.'" He got up from the sofa and began to pace the room. "That we have this chance—it's got to mean something. It's in my stars. I'm going to get that contract, and for the whole job, too. No splits."

"That's a pretty tall order," she pointed out, wondering what life would be like if he were disappointed.

"It's not an order, it's a reality. It already exists right here in my mind. So it doesn't really matter what they do; they can't stop the thing now. I have everything figured out. It's right. It's all right."

"Who are 'they'?" she asked. "Bruno and Whitman?"

He was staring out of the window, down toward the clove where the Cat River ran. It was the place where Marcia had died, but he was probably thinking of the river and the dam, and not of Marcia. When she mentioned Bruno and Whitman, he gave an impatient snort.

"I don't understand," she ventured timidly, "why you have to fight everything to do that now. You have your whole life ahead of you."

He turned to her angrily. "The dam is now, Angela. It's not in those years ahead. Quite obviously, if we don't make the bid, someone else will get it, and that's that."

"But what's so important? Is it the money? You have enough money. What do you want to become?"

An odd, secret smile. "Not money. Not expansion for itself. It's more than all of that. You wouldn't understand, because you think small, like the rest of them. It's a way of reaching out. Of getting into the system that runs things. After that—maybe there's something more than construction and contracting."

"But I thought you liked—"

"Just as I said, you don't understand. So let's drop it, okay?"

He was quite right: she did not understand. He refused to discuss it any further, but continued to work late, to come home cursing with frustration, and at the same time, to glow with a kind of wild excitement.

She worried about him, but knew he did not want her interfering with his life. She had her own to lead, and it was a busy one, with the baby's demands. As Michael grew less fragile, she often drove into town with him to visit Florence on her days off. She sometimes saw Betty, too, but Betty lived in chronic heartbreak at her own inability to bear a child. Angela felt guilty about taking Michael there, almost as though she were flaunting him.

The middle of October was approaching. The date loomed monstrously in her mind. It would be the first anniversary of Marcia's death. She wondered what it would mean to Glen. He gave no sign that it meant anything. Marcia was past, and the only thing he thought of now was the dam.

When the day came, she knew she could not be alone. She dressed early, packed the baby into his travel bed, and drove to Betty's house, knowing Florence would not yet be up.

The Betty who opened the door was a changed person, no longer quietly and wistfully brave, as she had been for the past year, but bubbling with happiness.

"Isn't it funny?" she exclaimed. "I was going to call you, and here you are." She scooped Michael from his mother's arms and carried him into the living room.

"Betty," said Angela, "don't make me guess."

Betty broke into a wide smile. "Did you guess? Would you believe it after all this time? It's true! I'm more than a month gone already. I didn't want to tell anybody till I was sure. It's due in June. Isn't that a beautiful month to have a baby?"

"Perfect. Just don't name it Katie June." They both laughed.

"Betty, I can't tell you. This makes my day. It makes my whole year, in fact." Angela took Michael from her and unzipped his bunting. "They'll be cousins. Won't it be fun? So close in age."

"I hope mine's a boy." Betty reached out to stroke Michael's tiny hand. "It'd be more fun for them if they were the same thing. How about some coffee?"

She went to the kitchen and filled her percolator. From the doorway, she said, "You know, I was really scared after those things you told me. Then when I kept wanting a baby and nothing happened—"

"Betty, why do you keep on with that? Don't you really have anything better to think about?"

"Well, it just seemed—"

"It just seems crazy to me. If you only knew what an amateur I was that night, you'd never dare take it seriously."

"Maybe not." For a moment, Betty looked undecided. Then came another delighted smile. "Angela, you don't know what this does for me. I've beaten the hoodoo. Now I really feel sure none of the other things are going to happen, either. Hey, I have to go to work in a little while."

"I know. I won't keep you. It's just that—you know what day this is, don't you?"

She didn't. Angela reminded her. For a moment, dismay shadowed Betty's face.

Angela explained, "I didn't want to stay home alone, especially when I can see the park from my window. But I'm so excited about you, I think maybe I can take it after all. That's what I meant when I said you've made my year. Maybe you've beaten my hoodoo."

"Do you mean your hoodoo was Marcia?"

"I hate to put it like that, but yes. It wasn't only seeing her die. It's Glen. Everything I've got was supposed to be hers. I keep thinking maybe I'll have to pay for it someday."

"Oh, come on. Nothing's going to happen."

They finished their coffee and Betty left for work. Driving home, Angela marveled at the transformation in her. Betty really did seem to feel she had broken a spell. And thank heaven for that. It was a spell that should never have been cast in the first place.

As she turned up the road toward Villa Fabiani, a car's

111

horn blasted on the hill above her. It was not a single blast, but screamed on and on, coming closer and closer. The sound hurtled down the hill, straight toward her.

She heard the screech of tires on a curve. Instinct, not conscious thought, made her drive off the road. She had no time to reach for Michael or jump from the car before a green sedan shot into sight, streaking down the mountain.

Frozen, she watched it fail to make the last bend on the lowest, steepest part of the hill. It seemed to rise and bound through the air, striking one of the concrete gateposts just below where she sat.

Bruno Fabian. She struggled from her own car, which sat tilted at a crazy angle in the ditch where she had run it.

Michael cried, shocked by the jolt. She picked him up and hurried across the road.

Bruno lay flung back in the seat, his neck twisted. The door beside him was jammed.

Even if she could have opened it, she knew it would do no good.

13

An ambulance took Bruno away. A tow truck removed his car, but in the concrete post, a large, green-tinted gash remained. Again Villa Fabiani lay under the hush of death.

It was exactly one year to the day since Marcia had died. And Angela had been a witness both times. She stayed in her room, cuddling little Michael for comfort. No one seemed to remember that she was there.

For once, she needed Glen's casual, almost mocking attitude toward death, but he did not come. Darkness fell and the afternoon ended. It was six o'clock, then seven. That was when they usually ate dinner. How could they even think of dinner?

Reluctantly she went downstairs. Ramona was seated alone at the table, waiting. When Angela came in, she said dully, "I'm sorry you had to see it, dear."

"I'm sorry it happened," was all Angela could answer. Whitman arrived, took his place at the table, and Stella began to serve.

No one seemed to have much appetite. After staring at his food for a while, Whitman said, "You know, it could be that Glen prefers the office at a time like this. It could be that he doesn't want to face all the emotion, including his own."

Ramona mumbled that it was possible. He asked, "How's Fay?"

"The doctor gave her something," Ramona answered. "I haven't wanted to bother her or the girls. Some of her relatives are there." She began to babble. "It's like a curse. First Tony, but then your father was getting on. Then dear Marcia, even though she wasn't a member of the family, but she would have been. Then Mike, and now Bruno. It's a curse. Poor Glen, he's had the most to bear."

Yes, thought Angela, he's had the most to bear, losing Marcia.

Ramona picked up her fork, but did not eat. "Why would his brakes suddenly fail, Whitman? How could it happen?"

"The police said something about the brake fluid leaking out," Whitman replied.

Angela exclaimed, "But that's silly! Even if there's a crack in the master cylinder, it would take a long time for the fluid to leak out. He'd have felt the brakes fading long before this."

There was silence. They stared at her, while the implication of what she had said hovered, not quite formed, in the air.

She wished she had not spoken. It was only that she knew something about cars and how they worked from her years with Ross.

"The mountain," Whitman said. "That long, steep hill. The more he pushed on the brake, the faster it leaked. It was the mountain."

Ramona murmured an agreement. For the rest of the meal she was silent, only raising her eyes from time to time to give Angela a long and thoughtful look.

They were finishing their dinner when Glen came home. He ate a sandwich in the kitchen, then joined the others for coffee.

"Okay, let's hear what happened," he said, accepting the cup his mother passed to him.

"Don't you know what happened?" Ramona asked in surprise.

"Of course, but I want the details. Maybe I should have said *how* did it happen?"

Whitman told him what the police had said about the failed brakes.

Glen shook his head. "That car was inspected just six months ago. You can't tell me they really look at those things. And what about the hand brake?"

"He might have panicked," Whitman speculated. "Maybe he didn't think to use it. Or maybe it couldn't hold, once the car picked up speed."

He hadn't panicked, Angela reflected. Not if he had the wits to blow his horn.

She watched Glen peacefully drinking coffee. He must have felt her watching. His eyes turned to meet hers with a strange, almost challenging look.

Flustered, she blurted what she had been thinking. "He saved my life. He blew his horn all the way down. He—even when he was—"

Glen continued to observe her, more soberly now. He needed no translation of her garbled remark. Someone must have told him she had been there when Bruno went down the hill.

He lowered his head and stared thoughtfully into his coffee cup. She wondered what he was thinking. About the failure of the brakes. About Bruno, dead. The accident that almost killed Glen's own wife and son.

The accident . . . accident . . .

She shivered. It was a terrible accident. And Whitman was right: the more he pushed on the brake, the faster it would leak. A cruel paradox, but she knew it could happen.

*   *   *

115

With Bruno's death, his workload had to be distributed among the survivors. That meant even longer hours, at least for a while. After the funeral, Glen went directly to the office and worked until one o'clock in the morning. It was the best time to work, when everyone else had gone, and there were few, if any, phone calls.

After a while his mind began to fuzz over with fatigue and he went home. He tried to be quiet, but he must have waked Angela when he turned on the bathroom light. He was staring, almost without seeing, into the mirror, when he heard her ask, "What's wrong now?"

"Nothing's wrong." He turned to look at her shadowy form on the bed.

"It's strange how things work out, Angela. There's only the two of us now. It's a hell of a thing to say, but I can feel it easing already. There's only Whit and me, and I think I can handle him."

"Handle him? How? About the dam?" She rose up to her elbow as he went into the bedroom.

"The dam is only one of the things, but it's the main one." He dropped his cuff links into a wooden dish on the dresser.

He was unaware that he had been smiling to himself, until she asked, "Glen, what would you do if Bruno hadn't died?"

He turned to her, glaring. "What are you talking about?"

"I just meant," her voice was small and timid, "because you said everything's easier for you now. But what if—" She stopped.

Very quietly, he replied, "You're forgetting something, aren't you, Angela? He was my uncle."

"No, I didn't forget. I know you'd rather have him alive— even if he disagreed with you." She snuggled down again, pulling the covers to her chin.

* * *

He continued to work at the same compulsive pace. He knew he was compulsive. That was the way he wanted to be. It left no time for reflection, for looking back, or anything but the job at hand. Even after he had sent in his bid, he worked, for there was much to be done, and the suspense of waiting for the opening of the bids was minimized if he kept busy.

He was sure he would get the job. He planned a trip to New York to discuss it with key people. Not officials, but key people. He told Angela about it when she joined him for an early breakfast one December morning.

"I'll be gone for a couple of days," he said. "I'd take you with me, but this is strictly business, and I don't know what you'd do with the kid."

Her eyes widened as she grasped his meaning. "About the dam? Glen, did you bid for it? Why didn't you tell me?"

He glanced toward the door, not wanting Stella or even his mother to hear. The fewer people who knew about it at this stage, the better, but Angela would be wondering anyway. You couldn't fool a girl who had worked four years in the business.

"Why didn't you tell me?" she asked again. "Does Whitman know you did it?"

"Of course he does. He's going with me. He's got his doubts, but that's too bad. We can't withdraw the bid."

"They didn't decide anything, did they?"

"It'll be a while before the bids are opened."

"Then why do you have to go?"

No, you couldn't fool a girl like her, but it was unfortunate that she knew how those things worked. She knew there was nothing he could do at this point.

"Angel," he sighed, "will you please just let me run my own business?"

"Your own? What about Whitman?"

"And that," he informed her, softening the reproach by pouring her another cup of coffee, "includes not questioning me."

She settled into a huffy silence, coming out of it only to wish him luck with his bid.

He thanked her, but he did not need her good wishes. He had more than luck going for him. Still, the whole conversation disturbed him. He would have to watch himself around this woman. Her questions were getting a little too penetrating. He had never imagined that she would be so well informed—about automechanics, for instance. Ramona, in baffled innocence, had told him of that strange remark at the dinner table.

Or that she would think so much. About anything.

14

Early the following Monday, Glen and Whitman started off
for New York. Wistfully Angela watched them go. She wondered if Glen would ever take her anywhere. Even staying
alone in a hotel room would have been a welcome change.
At least the view from the window would have been different.

She would have to content herself with Christmas shopping
in Kaaterskill. Taking the baby with her for companionship,
and because Stella and Ramona always seemed too busy
to babysit, she started down the hill in the ice and snow
remaining from an early winter storm.

She drove slowly, as she had done ever since the fatal
accident. On the road below, as though to remind everyone
of the tragedy, Bruno's car still sat in back of Sal's Service
Station, crushed and lifeless and shrouded in snow. She
wondered if they meant to keep it there forever. It seemed
almost indecent, when someone had died in the car. It was
like not burying a body.

That day, as she passed the garage, she was startled to
see two state troopers prowling about and poking under the
hood. Without thinking, she braked to slow down. Her car
went into a skid. She screamed as she spun and came to
rest in a snowbank.

Michael began to cry. She reached back to comfort him.

He was secure in his bed, probably only shocked by her scream and the sudden motion.

One of the troopers detached himself from Bruno's car. It was George Bennett, father of David and Zinnia.

"I'm okay, really," she said.

"You sure?" He helped her out of the car. "Now listen, honey, don't ever brake in a skid. Remember that, will you?"

She opened the back door and lifted Michael out. "I didn't. It was braking that made me skid."

He prodded the rear wheel with his foot. "Snow treads, but no chains. You oughta have chains, Angela, coming down that hill."

"I know." She was slowly recovering from the shock of the skid. "What are you doing with the car? Bruno's car? Is something wrong?"

"Just looking."

"But why?"

"Your husband asked us to, right after the accident. We couldn't find a thing the mechanics didn't find."

Glen? Glen had asked the police to investigate? "But—"

"Just thought we'd check it over one more time. Routine."

"I didn't know it was a police matter to begin with," she said, as a chill crept over her.

He grinned at Michael. "Cute kid you have there."

"Mr. Bennett—"

He tickled Michael under the chin and evoked a smile. She watched for a moment, then asked, "How's David?"

"Just fine," said George. "We got a letter last week. He's in Ecuador now, flying a helicopter."

"A helicopter!"

"Surprised us, too. They work around in jungles, you see. No way to travel except by air, no room to land a plane. It's pretty exciting, he says."

"I can imagine. And Zinnia? What's she doing?"

He shook his head in fond despair. "She's in New York. Working in a store, I think."

"Oh, are they back together?"

"Her and Ross? I don't think so. She just went there for a little fun. That girl's a great one for fun."

"Did she take the baby?"

"Nope, Katie's still with us. If you ask me, she's a lot better off with her grandma than with that scatterbrained girl." He nodded toward Michael. "Now you, you're a good mother. But you picked yourself a better man."

She felt a flush of resentment at the comparison. Ross had tried, but what could he do with a wife like Zinnia?

"I'll see you, Mr. Bennett. Send my love to David when you write, will you?"

She drove away, barely able to hold the steering wheel. Her hands felt watery. What were they doing, inspecting the car two months after the accident? What were they thinking?

She did not want to know.

She remembered that it was Glen who had asked them the first time. Glen . . .

It's all right, she told herself.

But it wasn't. They weren't satisfied. Why not? It made perfect sense, what Whitman had said: the harder he pushed on the brake . . .

Still, there should have been some warning. Something.

The next evening, Glen and Whitman returned from New York. They said little during dinner about their trip, but afterward they stayed downstairs together, talking. As if they had not already had two days to discuss it, Angela thought with some impatience. Later, when Glen joined her in their apartment, he was smiling to himself.

She asked, "What's the news about the dam?"

His smile disappeared. "How can there be any news? They haven't opened the bids."

"Something must have happened to make you look like that."

"Coming home to you, maybe?" He leaned across Michael to kiss her cheek. His manner, it seemed to her, was superficial and perfunctory. The thing that had been bothering her burst out.

"Glen, after Bruno died, did you ask them to inspect the car?"

"Ask who?" He sorted through the mail that she had set aside for him.

"Them. The garage. The police."

"Well, naturally. I was afraid they wouldn't think of it themselves." He tore open a letter that had no return address, although it was neatly typed on business stationery.

She was disturbed by his odd, bright look. "But why? Did you think—was it because you thought Sal wasn't careful during the safety inspection?"

He frowned intently at the letter. She could see only two short paragraphs, and wondered why it took him so long to read it.

"I saw them there yesterday," she went on. "The police, looking at the car. I asked Mr. Bennett, but he wouldn't tell me."

"Why should he?"

"I just wondered what they were thinking. When you asked them to look it over after the accident—what were you thinking?"

"Angela, dear, what would anybody think in those circumstances?"

A good question. She had no answer for it—at least none that she could tell him. All she had succeeded in doing was showing her curiosity about something she probably would have been better off not noticing.

She knew that many firms would be bidding for the job of building the dam. She had not actually believed Glen would get it, despite his confidence, until she saw it in his face. He came home early one night, which was unusual, and from the moment he entered their apartment, she knew.

"Did you—" she began as he came toward her. The rest of her question was lost in his embrace. He stood holding her, rocking on his feet. Then he eased her toward the bed.

"Glen, tell me."

His actions said more than if he had spoken. "Take off your shoes," she gasped as he smothered her face.

He whispered, "Shut up." Then he drowned out all sounds. Fleetingly she hoped he had locked the suite door, and then she was lost.

When it was over, he said into her ear, "I knew we could make it together."

"That's what we've been doing since—" No, he meant something else. He meant the dam. He was saying she had inspired him, that he had done it for her, but she knew better. It was for himself.

She sat up to kiss the back of his neck. "You still have your shoes on."

He did not reply. He was sitting on the edge of the bed, his face sober.

"Tell me about it," she said. "Is it all wrapped up?"

"Not quite. I didn't sign yet. It's Whit. He's trying to make them think we can't handle it. He's trying to get us disqualified. Do you know what that can do to the firm?"

She knew. She could not help thinking that maybe Whitman was right. It was too big a job for Fabian. But she knew how much it meant to Glen.

"They'll have to prove it before they can disqualify you," she said.

He turned to her, smiling. "Exactly."

She knew he would find a way. He never told her how he worked it out with Whitman, but by February, the contract was signed.

His life had fallen into place. Now that the pressure was off, he could spend more time at home. In some ways, he seemed to be making up for the nights and weekends he had been away. To her mild surprise, he even agreed to accept a dinner invitation with Betty and Tom. It was the first time he had ever done such a thing. His heavy work schedule did not allow for socializing, and there was also, she suspected, the fact that Tom was an employee.

Betty had left her strenuous job, but even without it, she was often tired. This might be the last time, she had explained, that she could entertain before her baby was born. She arranged a date for a Sunday early in March. Leaving Michael with his grandmother, Angela and Glen drove down the hill in brilliant sunshine and glaring snow.

"You seem happy," Angela remarked, noticing his pensive half-smile as he cautiously steered the car. "What are you thinking about?"

"I was thinking," he said, "that in a few years, snow like this will be running down the watershed to fill our reservoir. Do you know something, angel? I always liked water, ever since I was a kid."

"Funny that you should stay up here in the mountains. I should think you'd be drawn to the ocean."

"It's not the same. The ocean's just there, already made.

I'd rather live right here and build a dam, make my own water."

He parked in Tom's driveway, shut off the engine, and pulled her toward him.

Tom's garage door stood open. "Their car's gone!" she exclaimed.

A piece of paper had been stuck in the back door. She went to pull it out. The note was hastily scrawled, nearly illegible: *Gone to hospital.*

"Oh, God, no!"

"What is it?" he asked.

Sliding back into the car, she showed him the note. He turned on the engine and they drove off over the mountain toward Kaaterskill.

"I wonder what happened." She felt helpless and shaky. "It can't be her baby. She's not going to lose that baby!"

The hospital receptionist directed them to the waiting room, where they found Tom. He sat hunched, his face in his hands.

"Tom, what is it?"

He looked up. "I don't know. She started to hemorrhage. She thought the baby was coming. I don't know."

Angela sat down with him, but he could not tell her any more. He had no idea what was happening, only that it alarmed him and terrified Betty.

"Angela held his hand. "It's going to be all right, Tom. She wants that baby so much. It just has to be all right."

He made no response. She asked him to join them for coffee. He refused, wanting to be alone. Glen and Angela took an elevator down to the cafeteria.

As they drank their coffee, Glen said, "Betty's going to be okay, isn't she?"

"Probably she will be, but I don't know about the baby. It's so early."

"You had your baby early."

She was glad he realized it. There had been a time when she thought he doubted her.

"Yes, but this is too much. It's more than three months too early."

"Oh, really? Too bad, then."

The waiting had only begun. She did not see how it could take so many hours when the baby was so small, but Betty's labor was long and hard. Finally, at two o'clock in the morning, her son was born. At ten minutes past two, he died.

15

It was July. Glen estimated that in perhaps a year they could start to dig. True, it might take a little longer than that to move the people out of the valley, but the dam site itself was unoccupied. They could have begun the dam at any time.

And now this. He sat at his desk, the report in his hand, and pretended to read it. He already knew what it said, but he had to keep his eyes on something besides Whitman.

"I could sum it up for you," Whitman said. Glen did not miss the note of triumph in his voice.

"No need," he replied. "This thing is just a formality. It shouldn't surprise you any more than it does me."

"Now look, Glen." Whitman pulled over a chair and sat down. "You know what it means, don't you?"

The engineers had recommended a change in the type and style of the dam. Glen knew exactly what it meant. It was an extremely serious matter.

"It can throw off all our estimates," Whitman went on. "We've already got the contract on the basis of those estimates. And if—"

"Anything else you want to tell me?"

"I say we should disqualify ourselves."

"Yes, I believe you mentioned that."

"Don't you understand? We've got to. Right now, we're in a no-win bind. If we follow their recommendations, it louses up our estimates. If we refuse, this thing can end up in court, and that could drag on for years. We can't *afford* it."

Glen looked up from yet another reading of the letter. There was something in what Whitman had said—not the words themselves, but the inflection—that gave him an idea. He betrayed nothing, but only continued to watch calmly as his uncle sputtered.

"I knew we shouldn't have taken it," Whitman said. "A thing like this is just not for us."

"We shouldn't have taken it?" Glen repeated, as though mildly interested. How many times had he heard that song?

"Of course not. I told you even before we signed the contract. And now you'd better start listening. If the engineers recommend a different type of dam, you can bet there's a good reason. Hell!" Whit slammed the desk with the flat of his hand. "We can't change now. All the plans and equipment and materials— We never should have taken it in the first place."

"Let's skip the repetition," Glen said. "That could save some time. Now just exactly what do you propose at this juncture?"

"I propose—" The older man sighed, knowing already how his idea would be received, "to let them sue us for breach of contract."

Glen's eyebrows rose.

"What else can we do?" cried Whitman, his agitation growing. "That should annul the contract. They can do it, you know, if we refuse to go along with their instructions. Then at least we'll be out from under it."

Glen, still refusing to show any emotion, replied, "I can almost believe you mean that, Whit."

128

Whitman meant it, but Whitman was breakable. Glen was not.

Still, the problem loomed so hugely that when he went home late that night, he scarcely noticed Angela, awake to receive him as he climbed into bed.

"I've got something to tell you," she said, running her hand over his chest.

"Not now," he groaned. "People have been telling me things all day."

"Trouble at the office?"

"No, why do you ask? There's never any trouble at the office."

"Oh, Glen! Anyway, this is nice news. At least I hope it's nice."

"As long as it doesn't concern the dam."

"It doesn't. Just us. We're going to have another baby."

It took him a moment to adjust his thinking. Another baby. So now there would be two. He couldn't see that it would make as much difference in his life as the first one had.

From somewhere, he came up with a recollection of what prospective fathers were supposed to say. "Hey, that's great."

"Isn't it? We're really turning into a family. I hope it's a girl." She snuggled against him. He put his arm around her and continued to think about the dam.

She wondered if Glen was displeased. He hadn't seemed very excited, but naturally he had other things on his mind. A baby was only a footnote to his life. This might have been the time to ask about the house he was supposed to be building, but she dared not mention it. The house had fallen by the wayside, buried under dreams of the dam.

Still, she was lucky. She had more than most people could ever hope for, at least materially. And she had Michael, and another on the way. It made her remember the time she had gone to visit Betty in the hospital, after that horrible day in March.

"He's dead, Angela," Betty had sobbed about her baby. "He's dead and I wanted him so much. I had a name all ready for him. I named him Terrence, and I was going to call him Terry. I thought it was so cute for a baby—and now he's dead."

After that, Betty stayed at home and occupied herself with sewing shirts and bathrobes for Tom.

Donna Elizabeth Fabian was born the following February. With a newborn and a toddler, Angela found herself so busy that she was almost glad not to have the added responsibility of keeping a house.

The house, in fact, was not mentioned any more. Glen scarcely gave a thought to their living arrangements, or even to the children. His whole preoccupation was the reservoir.

It involved far more work than the simple damming of a river. Because it was being made to hold drinking water, the land had to be cleared of trees and buildings. Only stone walls and foundations were allowed to remain. Barns were burned and barnyards were dug deep to remove all contamination of the soil. Two cemeteries had to be moved.

During the spring, Glen made several trips to New York and one to Albany. Occasionally Whitman went with him, but most of the time Glen went alone. Their behavior toward each other was polite but cool, which made it seem as though the rift still existed, although neither would discuss the matter at home.

From time to time, Angela asked how things were going. Glen would mumble "Okay," but gave her no more information than that. And so, when rumors began to ripple through Burley's Falls, she did not, in the beginning, understand the full implication.

She heard it first from her mother. Monday and Tuesday were Florence's days off, and Angela would often take the children to visit her. She arrived at noon one mild day in April, bringing a package of hamburgers. After lunch they went out to the yard, where Michael romped with a neighbor's dog.

Florence sidled close to her daughter. "What's all this I've been hearing about Glen's uncle?"

"Whitman?" Angela asked in surprise. "How could you hear anything about Whitman? He doesn't *do* anything to hear about."

"It seems he does, according to Tom."

"What does Tom know about Glen's family that I don't know?"

"Plenty, I guess, if you haven't heard this." Florence lowered her voice. "Tom says that Whitman Fabian is in a lot of trouble. Some young man, a salesman or something, made a complaint."

"About what?"

"That Whitman Fabian—I don't know how to say this—that he made advances."

"To the salesman? Oh, Mother, that's not true!"

"How do you know? Of course he'd deny it."

"But he's not like that."

"You're not a man. You don't know what he's like with men."

"Just because he never got married, that's ridiculous."

"What reason would the young man have for saying a thing like that if it wasn't true?" Florence asked. "What would he get out of it?"

"I don't know. Attention, maybe."

"Who'd want that kind of attention?"

"You never know about people. Maybe he has his own reasons. Maybe he's the one with the problem, and—"

"I think it's sweet of you to be so loyal to the family," Florence said. "What does Glen say about it?"

"Glen doesn't talk about things like that."

"Not even to you?"

"Not even to me. And I still don't believe it." Angela concentrated on winding a blade of grass around her finger. She felt unaccountably ashamed, as though Whitman's disgrace somehow reflected on her.

That evening she watched to see what they would do. Glen worked late, as usual, but Whitman came home early. He was moody and silent during dinner, and afterward, took a bottle of vodka upstairs to his room.

She was feeding Donna when Glen arrived home. He nodded to her, hung up his jacket, and stood staring absentmindedly at the cold fireplace.

His silence unnerved her. She said, "I've been hearing some strange things around town today."

"Oh, you heard it?" A vague, uncomfortable frown crossed his face.

"What do you mean by *it*? I heard something, but I don't know if there's any truth in it. About Whit."

"Sticky, isn't it?" he said.

"But is it true?"

"How do I know? I wasn't there when it happened."

"If it happened."

"All right. If it happened."

"Who's the person that complained?"

"Nobody you know. Some equipment salesman. A new guy, Millard Hughes."

"Why does he have to make it public? That's so awful for everybody. For himself, too, I should think. And poor Whit."

Glen sat down, brushing a hand over his face. "Sweetheart, I don't know. I have no idea what went on or why. Maybe he had it in for Whit, you never know."

"Isn't there anything we can do?"

"If you've been hearing it all over town, it's kind of late to hush it up, don't you think? Hell, what a mess. I'm telling you, we don't need this."

"But if it were true—if he was really like that, wouldn't we know?"

"How would we know?"

"Well, from his past behavior. Or—it's an emotional problem, isn't it? He needs help, he doesn't need to be crucified."

"I don't know, dear, if it's an emotional problem. Some people say it is, some say it's perfectly all right, just different. I wish I could think of something." He became engrossed in looking through the mail, although usually he complained that it was nothing but ads.

Soon Millard Hughes's accusation became public knowledge. Whitman tried to ignore it, and went to the office every day as though nothing had happened. But he looked strained, and took to drinking in the evenings.

Angela found it almost unbearable. One morning at breakfast, after Whitman had taken a cup of coffee to his room, she said to Glen, "It really isn't fair, you know that? If somebody made a pass at a girl, all you males would think nothing of it, even if the girl didn't like it. Why does this have to be a federal case?"

"It's different, dear," he answered, "because this kind of thing is particularly offensive to a lot of people."

"Why particularly? Wouldn't it be offensive if he propositioned me?"

"It certainly would. I'd kick his ass right over into Massachusetts."

"Only because I'm your property, right? Not because anybody would care how *I* felt. Well, I don't see where this is different. Besides, it's my understanding that gays don't make passes at just anybody. It'd have to be somebody they're fairly sure of, exactly for this kind of reason."

"So what are you saying? That it didn't happen?"

"Maybe. Or maybe this Hughes person gave out some kind of secret signal that he's ashamed of."

Glen swallowed the last of his coffee. "This is getting rather convoluted, isn't it? You're a dear to be so concerned about Whit, but the matter is out of our hands. And there's no point in speculating on Millard Hughes's psychological makeup. We can't do a thing about it."

She thought there must be something they could do, some way to quiet Millard Hughes. Let him bring a suit for sexual harassment on the job, if he wanted, and stop spreading rumors. But Glen seemed tired of the whole issue. He only wanted to get on with the dam.

He worked regularly six days a week and often on Sundays. Only occasionally would he spend a few hours with his family. Even then, he was singleminded. Waking to a brilliant Sunday in May, he suggested to Angela that they take the children to visit "the site," as he called it.

"Don't you see enough of that?" She remembered the valley as it had been. She did not want to see it destroyed.

"Never enough. Come on."

He was in the bathroom showering when the telephone rang. It was their own number, and did not ring in the rest of the house. Angela picked it up.

A male voice asked for Glen. She offered to take a message. The voice said something that sounded like "Tell him Bill called."

"Bill?" she repeated.

"*Mill.*"

"Oh . . ." The name touched a nerve. "Is this Millard Hughes?"

The phone clicked and went dead.

A moment later, Glen came from the bathroom, wrapped in a towel. "Thought I heard it ring," he said.

"You did. It was for you. Somebody named Mill." She saw him tense. "Was it Millard Hughes? When I asked, he hung up."

Glen's face seemed at least a shade paler. "What the hell did you ask for? You had no basis."

"Glen, what is going on? Why should Millard Hughes be calling you at home?"

"How would I know? And what makes you think it was Millard Hughes?"

"There can't be too many people named Mill. I just don't know what you're so upset about, unless—"

"Who said I'm upset?" He whipped off the towel and began to dress. "Come on, let's go. Don't waste any more time. And ask Stella to pack a picnic."

The phone call still bothered her. She tried to put it out of her mind and enjoy the day. Glen was happy and carefree as they drove over the mountains and through passes until they reached the valley that would someday lie beneath the reservoir.

The landscape that she remembered was gone. The farms and houses and the little spired church had been leveled. The trees were cut down and the earth scraped and torn. Giant machines, bulldozers and diggers, stood scattered about in frozen motion. The valley had not been widely inhabited. Most of it was wild and rocky, cut through by the rushing waters of the Cat River.

"You won't have to build much of a dam for that little thing, will you?" she asked, watching the usually shallow

135

Cat, then bloated with spring rains, as it tumbled south and eastward toward the Hudson.

"By the time you're holding back all that water," he said, "when it fills the valley, you're going to need quite a dam."

She heard the pride in his voice and understood how he felt, even though she was sorry to see the valley go.

The day was warm and slightly hazy, with a mild south breeze. They ate their lunch, and Michael played on the rocks while the baby slept in her travel bed. When Michael grew tired, they started home.

As their car climbed into the hills, Angela looked back. "Does this mean everything's settled about the dam? All those engineering problems?"

"Finally."

"So it's full speed ahead? Glen, why don't you ever keep me up with these things? It's your whole life, and you never tell me."

"It wasn't pleasant."

"How do you mean? Did you persuade the engineers, or did they persuade you?"

"It wasn't pleasant, because Whitman tried to stand firm and let them annul the contract."

"And you wanted to build that dam no matter what. How did you talk him into it?"

"It looks," he said, wheeling too fast around a bend, "as if friend Whit has lost some of his clout."

"How come?"

"It's obvious, isn't it? He's over a barrel."

"But what's that got to do with it? He can still handle his job, can't he?"

"Look," said Glen, "the guys we deal with are tough. They're men. You don't know the kind of feeling that runs against something like that."

"It's none of their business!"

"That's not how they see it. They see him as a cancer."

"It's still only the word of one man," she pointed out.

"More than one man, dear."

"More? Do you mean he's been making advances to—a lot of people? I just don't believe it."

"Not a lot, but more than one. And I hate to say this, but it doesn't really make any difference what you believe."

She supposed it didn't. It was what the *men* believed that counted.

"Who are the others?"

"Guy named Stanley Morales—"

"Morales!" She laughed drily. "That's beautiful. Mr. Morals."

"You think it's funny?"

"I don't think anything about it is funny." She wondered how Glen could take it so calmly. If Whitman had a problem, it was already his private misfortune, but the scandal made it difficult for the family as well.

"Somehow I get the feeling that you're not entirely sorry he's in trouble," she said.

"What do you mean?"

"You know what I mean. If he wanted to stop you from doing the dam, and now he's powerless—that plays right into your hands, doesn't it?"

The car swerved as he turned to look at her. His lips were pressed angrily together. Then he smiled.

"I don't find it exactly inconvenient," he said.

"But why? Why isn't it bad for the whole company?"

He did not reply. She asked, "Are you encouraging Millard Hughes?"

"Encouraging him? How?"

"Don't play dumb. Are you?"

He looked at her again with a twisted smile that she did not like. "Angela, darling, you stick to your baby-tending and let me take care of the business."

She closed her eyes, again remembering the telephone call. She did not even want to think about what was happening.

That night it thundered. Half awake, she lay in bed, feeling the reverberations in her body. Lightning flashed white on the wall beside her.

Thunder, lightning, and in rain . . .

What was that? Thunder, lightning, and in rain.

Another clap of thunder. It woke Michael, who began to cry. She got out of bed and went to pick him up.

Probably she would have to hold him until the storm was over. She settled in a corner of the living room sofa. He continued to flinch each time the thunder crashed, but he had stopped crying.

In thunder, lightning, and in rain.

No, it was *or* in rain.

When shall we three meet again,
In thunder, lightning, or in rain?

The three witches. *Macbeth.* What had made her think of *Macbeth*? She had heard thunder countless times since high school, when she studied the play, and never thought of *Macbeth*. It was something else.

When the storm drifted away and the thunder stopped,

138

Michael fell asleep. She put him back in his crib and spread the comforter over him.

Donna was sleeping soundly, and so was Glen. Angela felt wide awake. Something seemed to be nagging at her. She knelt on the floor and searched the low bookcase between the two French windows until she found her old copy of Shakespeare's complete works. She curled up again on the sofa and began to read.

Not far from the beginning, she found what she was looking for. It was the prediction spoken by the witches when they first greeted Macbeth on the heath. It was the prediction, rather than the lines themselves, that seemed to tell her something. The prediction and what happened afterward.

All hail, Macbeth! Hail to thee, Thane of Glamis!
All hail, Macbeth! Hail to thee, Thane of Cawdor!
All hail, Macbeth! That shalt be king hereafter.

At that time, Macbeth was only the Thane of Glamis. All the rest, the witches were foretelling.

Were they, she wondered, telling what they actually saw for the future? Was it really meant to happen? It finally did, because Macbeth made it happen. And he made it happen because the witches had predicted it, planting the idea in his mind.

Did Shakespeare mean that it was predestined? Would it have happened anyway, even if Macbeth had sat back and done nothing? Or was it only because the prediction caused him to force fate, murder the people who stood in his way, that he became Thane of Cawdor and then King of Scotland?

Destiny? Or the power of suggestion? She skimmed through the rest of the play, trying to find an answer. Shakespeare had been perceptive about human psychology even before psychology as a science was invented. But she was not learned enough to fathom his purpose, as it pertained to Macbeth.

And what about Glen?

He wouldn't, she thought, just because of something I said. Yet, after Marcia's death . . .

The room was growing light. She closed the book and watched the sun rise.

16

The sky was a blaze of pink and orange, with blue-black clouds just above the horizon. She gazed at it, thinking how peaceful it looked, until the bedroom door clicked open.

Glen, in his pajamas, stood watching her. "What are you doing?"

"Reading," she said. "I had to comfort Michael during the storm, and I couldn't get back to sleep."

Michael woke soon afterward. He had completely forgotten the storm, and clamored to visit his grandmother.

In the middle of the morning, after Glen had left for work, Angela drove into the village. The day was warm and sunny, and Florence was out on her porch, painting a set of chairs.

"No, I don't want any help," she insisted. "I'm almost finished, and you can do your part by keeping the babies out of the paint. Of course you heard Tom and Betty are having another."

"No, I didn't hear." Along with her joy, Angela felt a momentary hurt that no one had told her. "When's it due?"

"Early January, I think. I wonder why she didn't tell you."

"I suppose she never forgave me for having these two, especially when—" There was more than that for which Betty might not have forgiven her. "I hope it's going to be okay."

"No reason why it shouldn't be."

"No, I guess not."

She watched Michael playing among the wildflowers and felt content. Betty would have her baby. Macbeth faded back into literature, as the night, which always brought worries, had faded into day. The world was a sane place after all. They spent a peaceful morning, ate a lunch of grilled cheese sandwiches on the porch, and then she took the children home.

Villa Fabiani was deserted in the early afternoon. Ramona was out at a hospital committee luncheon, and Stella and Albert had gone to visit their daughter. For once, Angela felt as though the house was really hers. She could breathe, stretch out, relax.

She put the children to bed for their naps, then wandered through an upstairs hall that was hung with paintings of the Hudson River region. She had always liked those paintings. They were a part of the world she knew, the craggy gorges and looming mountains of the Catskills. The waterfalls, the hemlock forests that had once covered the slopes.

She wished she could have seen the mountains then. A tragedy of the nineteenth-century tanning industry was the destruction of all the virgin hemlocks in the Catskills. When the last stand of trees had been cut down for its bark, the tanning industry folded and died. Only the inaccessible hemlocks, such as those at the bottom of Mile Gorge, remained.

At the end of the hall, the west stairway led down to a back vestibule and the library. Now, for a while, she could enjoy that, too, without the unshakable idea that she was trespassing.

It was not much of a library. Most of the books dealt with contracting and engineering. On the panels between the bookshelves hung photographs of Fabian projects. The Fabians had been everywhere. They had built hotels, schools, and shopping centers. They had built a cog railroad that once ran straight down the mountainside, and they had dug the lake at Mile Gorge Park.

But in all their years, they had never built a dam. Glen and Whitman would be the first.

A sudden sound made her pause and listen. It came from somewhere inside the house, a muffled snap, or crack.

She held her breath. It might have been someone breaking in. And she was alone.

She ran up the stairs to where her children lay sleeping. They had not wakened.

She looked out of her sitting room window, which faced the front of the house. A blue Volkswagen stood in the driveway. Whitman's car. She remembered how they had kidded him for buying a small car with no status value.

It meant he was home. She was not alone after all. Perhaps he had made the noise. She could not be sure.

The door to his suite stood open. The rooms were empty. She went back down the stairs, calling his name.

She ran from room to room, searching. There was no trace of Whitman, no sign of an intruder. Only that faint crack, and then silence. A feeling of clammy dread came over her.

Finally there was no place to look but the basement. The door stood ajar. She called softly into the darkness. Her only reply was the muted roar of the oil burner. But she felt a presence. She knew he was there. She turned on the light and started down the steps.

Whitman lay on the floor, his shattered face resting in a puddle of blood. His fingers were curled around the handle of a revolver.

She stared, and could not move. He was dead. There was nothing she could do.

She began to feel sick. His blood looked dirty, mingled with the filth of the basement floor.

If only she were not alone. She was always alone. How many times had she seen people die?

She looked up the police number and telephoned from the kitchen. She was surprised at how calmly she managed to report what had happened.

Always alone.

She ought to call Glen.

He was not at his office. They told her he had left for the dam site, but had probably not reached it yet.

The police arrived only moments before Ramona returned from her luncheon. Now there was someone else to handle it. Once again, funeral arrangements had to be made.

They were all gone, the old man and his three sons. All so quickly. The only one left was Glen.

You'll be running the business before you're thirty-five, she had told him. *Brilliant, early success. Running the business before you're thirty-five.* Her legs felt weak as she climbed the stairs to her suite.

Even with the door closed, she could not shut out what had taken place. *I don't find it exactly inconvenient.* Glen's words.

But Glen had not done this. Whitman had done it.

And yet—what else could Whitman have done?

17

After Angela's phone call, he tried to decide what to do. He concluded that there was more to be accomplished at the office than at home. For that matter, the entire firm would need restructuring, but good taste required a decent wait.

At five-thirty, he went home. He found his family gathered in the library, making plans. It was an exact replay of what they had done after Mike's death. And Bruno's. The endless conferences, and in those stiff old chairs. He hated walking into the middle of it.

"Hell," he said as they turned to look at him. "Just when we're ready to start the real work."

There was not much family left. Only Ramona, Angela, and Fay. He did not know why Fay had to be there. And he did not like the look on Angela's face. It was a look of wariness and reproach, and they were meant for him.

He shook his head in distress. Denial. "Hell," he said again.

Fay asked, "What made him do it?" She was asking the wall, and her voice was high and watery. He could not help thinking what a stupid bitch she was to have to ask that question at all.

He frowned, turned a chair around, and sat on it backward.

"It's pretty obvious, isn't it? Would you want to be in his position?"

From the corner of his eye, he could see Angela watching him.

"Like Angela said, it was nobody's business, but they hounded him."

To himself, he sounded properly self-righteous. Angela stared at the floor.

"And now," he added, "we're coming to the crucial part of the whole project. It's a filthy mess."

At that, she got up and left the room. He remained for a while with his mother and aunt, to discuss the funeral plans. Everything had already been decided, he found, but they pretended it hadn't. "Is that all right?" they asked him each time they mentioned a choice of music, or where to send the obituary. After a while he extricated himself and went upstairs to his apartment.

Angela lay on the bed, weeping. He thought the apartment seemed empty, and then realized the children were not there. Probably with Stella. It was just as well.

She looked up, her face streaming. "It's so sad, the poor man coming home to kill himself, all alone."

"It was his decision," Glen replied. "It's all over for him now."

She blotted her tears and stared at him. "For you, too, isn't it? The whole hassle's over with."

"I don't quite understand."

"All I know is, when this thing started, you said you didn't find it inconvenient."

"I didn't. Should I lie about it?"

She could not seem to think of an answer. He repeated, "As I said, the final choice was his. Death comes to everybody, angel. Don't you think it's better, in some ways, to be able to choose, than just have it happen?"

Not wanting to stand there and look at her, he began to wander as he spoke. He wandered across the carpeted floor to the window and looked down at the trees on the slope below the house.

Down at Mile Gorge Park.

Angela said, "I suppose he could have tried to ride it out. But things like that—"

She hesitated. Glen turned from the window.

"That's exactly my point. He had a choice. But there are other situations, other kinds of death, that are never chosen."

"Well, that's true." She must have known what he was thinking, for her voice barely emerged from her throat.

"Let me ask you, while we're on the subject." He tried to make it sound as though the idea had just occurred to him. "You think I should have done more for Whitman. Okay, but how did I know what he had in mind, and for when? But there's another death I'd like to talk about. And you were right there when it happened."

"You could say I was right here when this happened," she exclaimed bitterly. "And Bruno—"

"Yes, that's interesting, isn't it? But a little late in most cases, except the time I'm thinking of. Now what did you do for her?"

"Glen, you *know*. I told you I tried."

"You tried?"

"To pull her up. I almost killed myself trying to pull her up."

"And when you discovered you couldn't, what then?"

He could see by the way she looked at him that he had scored some kind of point. He had always wondered about that moment as he tried to relive exactly what must have taken place.

"She—slipped," Angela said fuzzily. "Out of my hands."

He took a step closer to her. "Just like that?"

"Glen, what has all this got to do with Whitman?"

"Oh, we're sticking to the subject of Whitman, are we? Well, it's only a matter of curiosity. I've been wondering, over the years. It seems a strange thing to happen, just falling off a cliff."

"The ground broke away. You could see it."

"A dangerous path, then."

"It was. Really. They've changed it since then."

"Yes, I know, dear. I've been over the police reports."

"You—what?"

"The police reports. I told you, it was a matter of curiosity."

"You don't believe me."

"I believe you as much as you believe me. You say you were an unwilling witness to a tragedy, and you couldn't do much to stop it. I say the same. And there we stand."

She blinked her eyes rapidly and looked away. He thought he had never been more attracted to her than he was then. He made a move toward her, but stopped. He realized he wanted to hurt her, not give her pleasure, and he must not allow himself to lose control.

She watched him turn suddenly from her, leaving her frightened.

Like Marcia. Frightened out of her mind. He had said that once, about Marcia.

I believe you as much as you believe me. She did not believe him. Did he know it? And did he, in turn, think she had deliberately sent Marcia to her death? She wondered if she could go on living with him.

But a few minutes later, he acted as though nothing had happened. And that night he made love to her, in spite of her distaste for it then. "Not now!" she protested, still seeing Whitman on the basement floor.

He called her "angel," whispering in her ear. The feel of

his lips on her ear had always been sensual. And she realized that she had probably misunderstood that earlier conversation. He must have been saying he was as innocent as she was.

Work went on as usual at the reservoir site. On the day of the funeral the men paused for one minute of silence, and that was all. Sixty seconds for Whitman Fabian. Then the bulldozers and power shovels roared again. They were digging to begin the dam.

The next Sunday came, as warm and bright as the previous one. She assumed that Glen would go to work, but apparently he was ready for another holiday, although not to the dam site again. It was even more ripped up than before.

"How about a cookout in the park?" he suggested.

She felt the color leave her face. "I'd rather not."

"Why? What's wrong? It's a perfectly good park. Only five minutes away. Costs only a couple of bucks to get in."

She did not need to mention that it had bad memories. They were every bit as bad for him, but he would not have considered that a reason for staying away. She packed a lunch of hot dogs and cole slaw, beer for Glen and Tab for herself.

She had not been to the park since Marcia's death, but found it less horrifying than she had expected. This was another year, another season, and these people were her own family. Marcia was long dead.

But looking at Glen, she thought: he wouldn't be here with me, these children would not exist, if Marcia had lived.

In one instant, a clod of crumbling earth had ended Marcia's life and changed her own completely.

She stared out over the lake that rippled in to shore, thinking of Whitman. His death was much fresher in her mind than Marcia's. Had Glen been an innocent onlooker,

149

as he claimed? She remembered the phone call from "Mill," and Glen's reaction to it. The comments and innuendos. And the success—made possible by Whitman's being "over a barrel."

No, she thought, he was Glen's uncle. They were a very close family.

And now they were gone—the two who had tried to stop him from building the dam.

Glen came back from a short walk with Michael, to find her still watching the lake. "What are you thinking about?" he asked.

"Just thinking."

"Well, rise and shine. Let's all take a walk."

"You just took one," she reminded him.

"That was nothing. We went over to the rocks and met a chipmunk that wanted a handout. Let's show Michael the forest, and the river. It's the Cat River, Mike. The one where we're building the dam."

"No, Glen."

"Why not? You said they moved the path. It's perfectly safe now, isn't it?" He picked up the baby and started toward the woods.

What was she afraid of? That her memories would overwhelm her?

If Glen could take it, she could, too. Glen had loved Marcia. But he hadn't seen the horror. Hadn't had to pull himself away from the clutching hands to save his own life.

What would he have done? she wondered as she followed him along the path. He might have been able to pull her up, or kept a cool head until he thought of a way to save her.

But he couldn't save Whitman.

And Bruno. What really happened to Bruno? Why didn't

anyone else think it strange that Glen's two uncles should both die suddenly in the prime of life? Perhaps no one else had heard Glen talk about the dam, and his destiny, and those who stood in the way of it.

Why, she wondered, isn't he afraid to have me know?

Maybe there was nothing to know. Maybe she was inventing the whole thing.

Michael let go of her hand and toddled ahead of her. Ahead—where Marcia had been. But Glen was there. He would not let anything happen to Michael.

Nor would he have let anything happen to his uncles. Not Glen, in spite of the things he said.

He stopped and looked down into the ravine. "It was here, wasn't it?"

"Yes," she said. "That's the old path. You can see how close it goes to the edge, and that's where it broke away. And there's the root she caught hold of. It's part of the tree. I threw myself around that tree, but all the ground is sloping here, and I started to slide, and it was crumbling . . ."

The earth had eroded still further in the intervening years. She wondered how long the tree could remain perched on the edge of the precipice. She feared for the tree, having to look down at those hemlocks forever, while the ground beneath it fell away.

"Maybe trees don't mind," she said.

"What are you talking about?"

"Don't mind—if they die." Why had he brought her here? Did he only want to see it? Or was he trying to remind her that he believed her as much as she believed him?

She started edging back along the path. "Now you've seen it."

"Now I've seen it." His eyes seemed to glitter, as though with fascination. Or was it tears? It frightened her.

In another instant, the wild light had gone. She was not sure it had ever been there. He was only her husband, carrying their baby in his arms, and grieving for a girl who was dead.

18

Throughout the summer and fall, work went on at the dam. Glen, eager to see it finished, pushed his men to the limit. There were a few complaints, but they were scarcely more than grumbles, for the overtime pay was generous.

The accountants at the Fabian office cautioned him. "We're going to use up our whole budget before the thing's finished, with all this overtime.

"Think about it," Glen replied. "The sooner it's finished, the sooner our expenses are finished. Simple arithmetic."

"You're forgetting something. We're talking about *double* overtime."

"Not to mention inflation and escalating costs. It all evens out."

It did not even out, but there was no arguing with Glen. He was the entire firm now.

When cold weather arrived, the work slowed, but did not stop. Men were laid off and there were more complaints. But those who did not lose their jobs were happy to have work at all in the wintertime.

In January, Betty and Tom became the parents of a daughter, a healthy, full-term baby. After Tom called to tell her the news, Angela celebrated alone with a glass of sherry.

The next day she went to the hospital to visit. Betty was

sitting in bed, looking content, and reading a book on baby care. Angela kissed and congratulated her.

"It's so exciting! I'm awfully glad it worked out this time. You'll have a dozen more. What are you going to name her?"

"Maria," said Betty.

"Oh. Any particular reason?"

"I like it."

"Yes. It's pretty."

In her mind, Angela saw the name written. Except for one letter missing, it was "Marcia." But she was the disturbed one now, seeing "Marcia" where there wasn't any Marcia.

Betty asked, "How's everything going for you?"

"Okay, I guess. Nothing different. The kids are fine. They keep me busy. I'm practically a widow, you know. A dam widow. No, that doesn't sound right."

Betty laughed for the first time in almost two years, and Angela thought, She's happier than I am.

With the coming of spring, a full work schedule was resumed. Men who had been laid off were rehired, and new men were taken on. Until that time, most of the work had consisted of building temporary structures to divert the water around the portion of riverbed where the dam was to be erected.

By early spring, they were ready to lay out the broad base of the dam itself. From there, it would rise to nearly two hundred feet in height. It was to be a quarter of a mile long, with a top wide enough to contain a two-lane roadway and a body strong enough to hold back twenty billion gallons of water.

During the height of the season, Glen spent many nights at his cabin, which was only a few miles from the construction site. Michael often asked about his father. So that the children

154

would not forget him, Angela sometimes took them to visit him in his field office. He had little time to bother with them, but the children gloried in the wilderness of rocks and machines, and the reservoir, which was already beginning to fill.

With various incentives, Glen urged his men on to greater productivity. His impatience paid off. The dam took shape rapidly. It looked as though he might achieve his goal of having the major part finished before winter. Glen and his entire project seemed blessed—until one day in October.

It was a golden day, crisp, but not cold. During the mild afternoon, Angela played with her children on the back lawn, where Ramona had installed an elaborate gym set for them. Michael, who was three years old, was showing off what he could do on a trapeze, while Angela pushed his little sister in one of the swings. Inside the house, a telephone rang.

A few minutes later Ramona came out, looking dazed and bleak.

Angela asked, "Is anything wrong?"

"Something's very wrong," Ramona answered. "There's been an accident at the dam."

"Oh, no! Is it Glen?"

"Not Glen. Thank heaven for that. It was some of the workmen. One dead, and I don't know how many injured."

"Not—my brother?" Angela felt suddenly weak.

"Your brother?" Ramona had forgotten about Tom. "I shouldn't think so, they probably would have told me. I just thought you should know. This won't be easy for Glen, poor boy. He's had so many troubles."

Ramona had not been sure about Tom, or even interested. They'd tell Betty, Angela thought, and went into the house to call. There was no answer. That worried her still more.

She could not sit around doing nothing. She had to be

there, to know what had happened. Leaving her children with Ramona, she drove the many miles to the dam site.

Glen was not in his field office. No one could tell her where he was, although they were able to assure her that the dead man was not Tom. It was a name she did not recognize.

"What happened?" she asked one of the men standing in the doorway of the office.

"Part of the new work collapsed," he said. "They're still clearing it away. We think another man may be under there."

She hurried down the truck ramp, as near to the scene as the security guards would allow her. The injured men and the body of the dead one had already been taken away. Cranes and bulldozers were removing the debris that possibly covered another man. A sizable section of the stonework had fallen. It would take a long time to dig under all of it.

Crowds of sullen-faced workmen stood by observing the rescue. Several police cars had driven down the ramp into the work area. Angela looked for Glen, but could not find him. Nor did she see any sign of Tom.

Four-thirty came. Gradually, amost unwillingly, most of the men left for home. Although it was still day, the sun's rays were cut off by the encircling hills. Large, truck-mounted floodlights were brought in. Amid gathering shadows, the heavy machinery ground on, hoisting huge concrete blocks, pushing away rubble. Angela watched, transfixed, hoping a miracle would happen. The man might have been trapped in a pocket, protected from the weight of the fall.

She caught sight of Glen. He was yards away from her, talking with one of the foremen. He looked in her direction but gave no sign that he saw her.

A figure in a gray uniform moved away from the crowd and came toward her. It was George Bennett.

"How are you, Angela? Terrible thing, isn't it?"

"I don't see how it could happen," she said. "A dam tapers to the top. How could it just fall like that?"

"I'm not an engineer, dear. I think maybe they were going too fast. The stuff wasn't set. All I know is, it's too bad."

"Mr. Bennett, have you seen Tom? My brother?"

"No, I haven't, but I guess he's all right. I didn't hear of anything happening to any Burley's Falls men."

A few of the policemen left, but George remained, watching with her as a power shovel nudged at the massive chunks of concrete.

Progress was slow, and she was afraid of what they might uncover, but could not leave.

"Do you hear from David?" she asked.

George beamed. "Yes, he's doing fine. He's out in Texas, you know."

"I didn't know. Is he back permanently?"

"Yes, back from the wars, you might say. He ought to be coming home soon."

"I'll be glad to see him. And how's Zinnia?"

"Zinnia's married again," he said. "She did all right this time. Married some money. They're traveling in Europe right now."

"And you still have the baby?"

"Yep, we have her. She's a good kid, but it'll be easier on her grandma if Zinnia decides to take her back."

At that moment a hoarse cry went up from the rescuers. Angela turned and quickly looked away. Again she had seen death. Horrible, mangled death.

In the chaos that followed, she pushed her way toward Glen. Several times she lost sight of him. Then he would reappear, always, it seemed, farther away from her. When she finally reached him, he was talking with a group of people and had no time for her.

157

She caught his arm. "Glen, tell me, is Tom all right?"

He gave her a gentle shove. "Go on home."

"I have to know. It isn't Tom, is it?"

"No, it's not Tom. Now go home. You don't belong here."

"I do belong here. This is my life, too. I want to know what happened."

Again he tried to shake her off. "How do I know what happened? Somebody got careless and the thing collapsed."

"What do you mean?"

"Just what I said. It was a stupid accident." He lowered his voice. "These guys work with their backs, not their brains. What do you expect?"

She stared at him, waiting for a denial. But he meant it.

And it could have been Tom. Whoever it was, someone loved him. She pushed her way back through the crowd.

He was upset. He wouldn't have talked like that if he weren't upset.

She reached her car and found her hands shaking as she turned the key.

The mountain road was half lost in twilight. The trees on either side loomed shadowy and oddly threatening. Dusk— it was the loneliest time of day. The death of day. She felt that if anything should happen to her now, she wouldn't care, except for her children.

But nothing would happen. Not even the drowning predicted in her hand. She would live on and watch other people die. And somehow, horribly, she would be connected with those deaths. With Marcia's and Bruno's, because she had been there, and Whitman's, because she had been the one to find him. With little Terry's, because he was her nephew, and her father's, because he was her father. And with those two workmen, because Glen was her husband.

It was dark when she reached Burley's Falls. Instead of going home, she drove to Tom's house. His car stood in the

158

driveway. For the first time that afternoon, she felt glad about something. She knocked at the door. Tom answered, his face harrowed. He brightened when he saw her, but his welcome seemed forced.

She asked, "Can I come in? I wanted to be sure you were all right. I went over there, and nobody would tell me anything."

"You went all the way there? What for?"

"I was worried about you." Not about Glen, as he probably expected.

"Come on in," he said in a tired voice.

As they passed through the kitchen, Betty shot her a look of unconcealed hostility.

It caught Angela by surprise. "What's the matter?"

"It could have been Tom!"

"That's exactly what I thought. Why do you think I was worried?"

"Why should you care? Glen's getting rich while other people get killed."

Tom said soothingly, "Betty, not now," but he made no real effort to quiet her.

"It's not so much the money," Angela said. "He's not getting any huge amount of money for it. I mean, he has a lot of expenses, especially with all the overtime—"

"That's just the trouble," Tom interrupted. "All that overtime. Rush, rush, rush. Sure the guys like overtime pay, but when you start having accidents—"

"What do you mean?"

"They're working too fast."

"Tell me what happened. Nobody would tell me."

"I didn't see it happen. I was driving down the ramp with a load of sand and suddenly the guys started hollering. Then I saw the whole section coming down."

"But what made it come down?" she asked.

159

"Working too fast. Somebody told me it wasn't braced properly, and it wasn't set. They were climbing on it before it was ready."

"But didn't they know better? Didn't the foreman know better? The engineer in charge?"

"Your husband," Betty spat at her, "wants that job done so fast he's paying all the foremen big bonuses."

Angela gasped. "I didn't know that."

"It's true. Isn't it, Tom?"

He looked uncomfortable. Angela tried to explain. "I never even see Glen. He's always up at the dam."

Betty said, "Tom, I want you to quit that job right now."

"Come on, Bet, I drive a truck. That's safe enough."

"How do you know the whole dam won't fall on your truck?"

He shrugged. "You never know when you're going to get it. It's gotta come sometime."

His resignation only fed her fury. She was building to another outburst when Angela said quickly, "I'm really sorry. I wish you wouldn't be angry at me. I feel just as bad as you do."

"Why should you?" Betty snapped.

Halfheartedly, Tom offered a round of drinks. Angela declined and left for home.

19

For a while after the accident, Glen stayed away from home. It seemed pleasanter not to have to hear all the questions, hers and Ramona's. He spent the nights in his cabin, where he could have peace, and the days in his field office, where he was badgered by engineers, but being an engineer himself, he could handle them.

The cabin became less appealing as the temperature dropped. And when a howling wind rose one night, he weighed it against the small wood-burning stove and lack of insulation and opted for home.

Besides, he wanted to feel her body again. She must have gotten over her questions by now. It never ceased to amaze him, all those questions. She was untrained in most areas. How did she even know to ask such things?

She was awake when he slid into bed beside her. His heart tightened as she asked immediately, "Glen, have they got it repaired yet, or what?"

Damn. He lay on his back, staring into blackness. "What do you mean, 'or what'?"

"I mean, do you have to do the whole thing over again, if something was wrong with it?"

He gritted his teeth. The eagerness he had felt as he

drove home turned to coldness. He would have been better off in the cabin, where the cold was only external.

"There's nothing wrong with it. What the hell?" His voice was harsh. He could feel her withdraw.

But she persisted. "Then what made it fall? Or was it true, what I heard, that they were working too fast and it wasn't set?"

"Who'd you hear that from?"

"Various people. But why, Glen? Why so fast? In the long run it's not going to make any difference, and it will be a better dam, and safer for the men."

"Angela, dear, it doesn't concern you."

The bed jerked as she sat up.

"It does. Not only because of you, but one of the workmen happens to be my brother. And believe it or not, I care what happens to people, even if they aren't my brother."

"You do, don't you?"

Another tremor in the bed. "And you really don't. As long as you get what you want, you don't care what happens to anybody else. You're willing to sacrifice those workmen, even your own uncle. I don't know, Glen. You've turned into—something. I just don't know."

He was glad of that final sputter. It showed her weakness after all. *This is it, my girl. This is the end.*

She would have to go. He did not yet know how or where. She had to go, but at all costs, he would keep the children.

"Turned into what?" he asked. It might not be wise to keep talking about it, but he wanted to know exactly what she thought.

"Macbeth."

It took him by surprise. "That's really poetic. Not bad for a girl who never went to college."

"You get *Macbeth* in high school," she reminded him, and then asked, with a sarcasm of her own, "So I take it

162

everything's proceeding normally at the dam? Only a slight setback?"

"Of course it's proceeding normally. What did you expect?"

Got to go. He rolled onto his side, where he could no longer feel her warmth. His desire had gone. Maybe another time. Wanting her had nothing to do with the fact that she must go.

But how to effect this departure of hers? He would have to think of something. It might take a while. In the meantime, she couldn't prove anything, whatever she might say. It was only this endless questioning that ground away at him.

She lay awake, frightened at what she had said. She ought not to have let him know her thoughts. He had already warned her once.

Beside her, he breathed easily. The sleep of the innocent. Maybe she was all wrong about him. Maybe it really had been a careless accident on the part of the men themselves. Maybe Whitman really had gotten himself into a bind and then taken what he considered the only way out.

Maybe.

Why was she so determined to think he was guilty? Just because he had a crooked finger?

In the morning, he woke her. There were no kisses, no endearments. He took her quickly, with savage nips that made her cry out and finally slap him.

In spite of the bites, she felt a passion that seemed to have grown with time and with the troubles they both faced. She whispered, "Glen," and then, inadvertently, "I love you." He made no response.

After that, he came home more frequently. Enough so that, when she developed a queasiness that continued day after day, she thought she might be pregnant.

Soon she discovered she was not, but the nausea and

dizzy spells went on and on. Twice it became so bad that she had to leave the table in the middle of dinner. The second time it happened, Ramona went up later in the evening to see her. She placed a hand on Angela's forehead.

"It feels a little warm. It must be some kind of low-grade infection. Have you seen a doctor?"

"Oh, good heavens, it's not bad enough for a doctor," Angela replied. "I'm just under the weather."

"But it seems to stay with you. I don't understand."

"These things can drag on."

When it had dragged on for a few more days, Ramona suggested that she might find life easier if she went to stay with her mother for a while.

"Then you can rest. You wouldn't have the children to worry about. Stella and I can look after them. They're having a marvelous time with Stella right now."

Since Angela's sickness began, the children had been spending more and more time with Stella. Angela had scarcely realized it, had only been glad they were not around with their incessant demands and noise. Now, suddenly, their absence seemed a threat. They were being taken away from her.

"I'll be all right," she told Ramona. "And I certainly wouldn't want to leave the children."

She tried to pull herself together and resume her responsibilities, but the children were no longer interested in her. They would run to Stella as soon as they were dressed in the morning, and stay there nearly the entire day.

Then Glen himself suggested that she go to her mother's for a rest.

"It wouldn't be a rest," Angela told him, as a small, nameless fear flickered inside her. "She's alone, and she works. I'd feel I had to do things around the house that I don't have to do here."

164

"But you wouldn't have the children," he argued. "That's the hardest part, isn't it?"

She could not think of anything to say. It seemed as though they were trying to separate her from the children, and she did not know why. She only knew that she had been afraid of Glen ever since Whitman's death. Afraid, but not really knowing, and so she had refused to recognize it.

I've got to get away, she thought. Get away—and take them with me.

The next morning, before they could leave her, she asked them, "Michael, Donna, would you like to go to Grandma's house for a few days?"

Michael paused in his flight toward the door. "With you? Would we sleep there?" After a moment's consideration, he shook his head. "No, I want to stay here. I like Stella."

And Donna echoed, "Stehwa."

"What's so exciting about Stella?" Angela wanted to know. "Why is that more fun than Grandma's house?"

Michael shuffled his foot. "Because . . ."

"I suppose she gives you anything you want? What do you do there?"

He ducked his head and would not elaborate. Donna flapped her hands excitedly. She would have spoken, but Michael took a menacing step toward her.

Whatever it was, they must have been instructed not to tell Mommy. Angela could hardly believe it would be anything serious. Probably only a few bad habits that made life easier for Stella, such as television by the hour. That would captivate children, and Stella's television was a large color console, while Florence clung to her old black-and-white set.

Without the children, she refused to go. The children would not have minded, but she was apprehensive. There had been too much insistence on her leaving. Too much for her to believe it was all in her best interest.

Instead, she visited a doctor in Kaaterskill. He could find nothing specifically wrong with her, which, in itself, made her feel better. She discounted the sickness as "just one of those bugs that hang on."

A few days later she felt well enough to drive herself again to Kaaterskill. She managed nearly an hour of Christmas shopping before she became weak and shaky and had to return to the car. She sat for a while until the spell passed, and then she started home.

At Sal's, she stopped for gas. A familiar figure was bending over the open hood of another car. When he straightened, she recognized David Bennett. She opened a window and called to him.

"Angela Dawn!" A huge grin spread over his face. "How are you? You're looking okay. And by the way, congratulations."

"What for?" She was pleased to hear that at least she looked okay.

"You got married, didn't you?"

"Oh, yes. Thanks. You're only about four years late with that. David, it's great to see you. I heard you were doing some dangerous stuff. I'm glad you're okay."

He laughed. "Who said I wouldn't be?"

"Well, you know. All those air currents and things. You'll have to tell me about it sometime. Can we get together? Come and visit me up at the house."

"Aw, I'd feel funny up there. I'll see you around. How's Glen?"

"All right, I guess. He practically lives at the dam. I guess you've heard about the dam?"

It was difficult not to have heard about the dam. He knew of the accident in October and had heard that they were having labor troubles, which Angela had not known.

She could not ask him how serious it was. She felt ridiculous, not knowing about it. Glen had said nothing, and Tom and Betty had not been in touch with her since the accident. She mumbled that they would probably work it out.

"Well, I'll see you, Angela." He gave her a jaunty salute and went back to his own car.

By the time she reached home, her stomach was churning and her head reeling. She should not have gone out. But how long could she go on not living?

The sickness came and went. She had alternating periods of feeling better and feeling worse. On one of her good days she went to visit Florence, and learned that the men at the dam were talking of a strike.

"Something about shorter hours," Florence explained, "and better safety."

"That's understandable," said Angela. "But I thought he was giving them pretty generous overtime."

"Maybe. What gets me is they never had that dam all these years, so why does it have to go up so fast? Is it some kind of emergency or something?"

"Not as far as I know," Angela replied. "Only for Glen."

The following Monday, Glen set off on another trip to New York. He planned to be away for three days. "And when I come back," he told her as he left, "I expect you to be all over this thing."

She thought there was something odd in the way he said it. Something that did not sound entirely genuine, but she had long since ceased to believe that she understood Glen.

They did their best for her while he was gone—or seemed to. The children all but moved into Stella's suite, spending their nights as well as days there. They considered it an adventure. Angela had nothing to do except rest, and rest did not seem to help her. The nausea had lessened, and she could eat a little more than usual, but she felt weak and unfocused most of the time. After a spurt of activity designed to show them how well she was functioning, she would collapse on her bed for several hours. It occurred to her that another doctor's opinion might be a good idea, but she did not feel like exerting herself to go to one, even if someone were to drive her there.

On the night before Glen was expected to return, she woke suddenly in pitch darkness. She woke because she was suffocating. For a moment she thought it was part of a dream, but even awake, she lay struggling for breath. Her brain was gripped with dizziness, not in the usual lightheaded way of her illness, but as though all the blood had drained from it and she was about to lose consciousness.

Finally she managed to turn her head. She saw billows of smoke rising from the floor. She struggled to move over a few inches and looked down.

Inexplicably, there seemed to be a bottle of champagne in a silver bucket just below her. A champagne bucket, with ice. She continued to stare and wondered if it was real. Or was she dreaming? Champagne out of nowhere, and in the dark.

And steaming. Hot, instead of cold. She wanted to reach out and touch it, but could not move her arm.

Steaming. That was no ordinary ice in the bucket. It was dry ice. Frozen carbon dioxide, melting next to her face. And she was breathing it. Dying, without oxygen.

Again she tried to move. Something held her down. A paralysis. She tried to call out. Her body was not hers any more. She could not control it.

This is a dream, she thought. A dream.

But deep inside, she could feel herself dying. It was too real to be a dream.

She caught her breath and held it. She must concentrate—

168

every bit of her. Gather herself up and put it into one great effort. Roll over—over—over—

It seemed to take forever. After a long time, she thought she felt her head begin to move, and her shoulder. That, too, must be part of the dream. It couldn't really move, this great, insentient lump that was Angela.

She felt the cool sheet against her cheek and then slipped into unconsciousness.

In the morning she woke, lying on her stomach with her face to the wall. Something terrifying had happened. She could not remember what it was.

And then it came back to her. She found she could move with no difficulty and turned over to look at the floor.

The bucket was gone.

Of course. It had never been there. It was only a nightmare. But why would she dream a thing like that?

She fell asleep again, breathing easily. She wondered that she had ever taken breathing for granted.

She woke an hour later and got out of bed, testing herself. No nausea this morning, but she felt weak. She was starting to put on her bathrobe when someone opened the door to the suite. She thought it must be Michael.

It was Glen.

Surprised, she asked, "What are you doing here?"

"I live here," he answered. "How's everything?"

"Okay." She assumed he meant herself. "When did you get back?"

"About two. I didn't want to bother you."

He had slept somewhere else in the house, he said, and had only come in to shave and change his clothes. After a quick breakfast, he drove away to the office.

While she, who had had a whole night of sleep, could only return to bed after a cup of mint tea.

Glen was home relatively early that evening, at eight

169

o'clock, just as dinner ended. Angela had forced herself to eat and was looking forward to being alone in the apartment where she could fall into bed without anyone knowing.

But Glen said, "I brought you a Christmas present. Let's have a little party, you and me. In the main living room," he added as she started toward the stairs. "They've got a fire going. It's very nice."

She could hardly refuse without admitting that she still felt sick. Besides, it was rare and touching that he wanted to spend some time with her. To celebrate his homecoming, she supposed.

He sent her ahead of him into the living room. She took a chair beside the fire, which purred and crackled pleasantly. A few minutes later Glen came in carrying a tray with two glasses and a bottle of champagne.

A feeling of horror wrapped itself around her. A memory of not being able to breathe. It was the same bottle she had seen in her dream—if it was a dream.

It could not have been anything else.

Yet it was the same bottle. She knew, because she had seen part of the label. The top line on this label was identical.

"Something wrong?" he asked as he set the tray on the coffee table.

"No, I was just surprised. I didn't know we were going to have champagne."

"Why not? I said it's a party, even if we didn't invite anybody. It's an uncrowded party."

She wanted to ask where he had gotten the bottle. *When* he had gotten it. She could not think what to say. The whole thing sounded insane and was probably a dream after all.

Or maybe he himself had put the bottle in their room, perhaps wanting to celebrate then and there, but she had been too sound asleep. He might not even have thought of the danger of dry ice.

He popped the cork and filled their glasses. It was dry champagne, its tartness refreshing. It was exactly what she needed.

After Glen had drunk half a glassful, he picked up a brown paper package that had been lying on the table.

"Sorry this isn't gift-wrapped," he said, "but you know me. All thumbs when it comes to ribbons."

"Why not wait till Christmas?" she asked.

"Because I want you to have it now."

As she removed the wrapping, she could feel the object inside. A book. She almost knew what kind of book it was.

Then it lay on her lap. It was more or less what she had expected, although, unexpectedly, it was a rare old edition. *The Language of Cheirosophy.*

She felt leaden. She had wanted to be finished with cheirosophy. And he was Macbeth . . .

He fed on it, she realized. Fed on what she had told him, years ago.

She hid her distress and turned the pages, managing to delight in the book itself, if not the contents.

"It's beautiful, and thank you. It's kind of a—a memento."

"I like the things you told me," he explained once again. "And it's all happening, isn't it?"

"Not everybody's fortune was good," she replied. "And yours is happening because you're making it happen."

"What do you mean by that?" The change on his face in the dancing firelight was almost imperceptible.

"I mean the way you keep pushing ahead with the dam. You don't sit back and wait for it to happen; you make it happen."

"How else is it going to get done? Dams don't grow by themselves."

It was not what she meant, but she was glad he did not pursue it. She finished her champagne and he sent her to bed, while he remained downstairs with the rest of the bottle.

The next day she looked through the book more thoroughly. She found it not as readable as the one she had bought for herself. The print was small and the photographs blurry. A week later, on a rare day of feeling fairly well, she took it to show her grandmother when they celebrated Lydia's seventy-sixth birthday, and accidentally left it there.

She continued to feel better as the Christmas holidays arrived. She almost dared hope she had shaken the illness at last—the "bug," as she called it, or the "virus." But during the first week in January it all came back, the uneasy stomach, the bad taste, the dizziness and weakness.

It had only been the excitement of the holidays, she decided. A psychological recovery. She would die in that house. Probably it was a rare form of cancer, which the doctor had not recognized. She visited another doctor who gave her several prescriptions, none of which seemed to have any long-term effect.

The winter was cold, windy, and depressing, and she was alone most of the time. She rarely saw the children. She almost never saw Glen. Construction on the dam had slowed during the winter, but there were other problems. There were work slowdowns not caused by the weather. There had been anger and discontent ever since the accident.

In March, the labor troubles came to a head. By then the snow was melting and the work progressed at a rapid rate. In a few months, Glen expected the dam to be finished. The reservoir was already a sizable lake.

He was seldom at home, but came in one night while

Ramona and Angela were at dinner. Fay, as she often did, had joined them.

Glen did not come alone. Angela, her head gripped with dizziness at the moment, saw two figures appear in the doorway. She looked again. She did not want any strangers there when she was not at her best.

As they came into the room, she saw that the other was a young woman with frizzy blond hair. The two stood out strangely in a room that wavered as though under water.

Glen said, "This is Flora Bernhofer, my treasured assistant." His eyes swept over Angela. She tried to steady herself, but had no strength to react. Ramona and Fay, clearly taken aback, each murmured a greeting. Then they, too, turned to look at Angela.

Stella came from the kitchen to set places for Glen and Flora. Angela wondered vaguely whether the girl would spend the night, and where she would stay. And whether Glen would stay with her. She did not really care. She only wanted to be upstairs in her own bed right now, with everyone leaving her alone.

Glen said, "We had quite an eventful day, didn't we, Flora? I got backed into a corner and had to do something my wife will never forgive. I fired her brother."

Angela's hand was on her water glass. She felt its coldness seep through her.

"Fired—Tom?"

"Tom. Yes. I thought you'd remember the name. It was quite a disaster all around, wasn't it Flora? I brought Flora home with me because we have a lot of work to do in the wake of all this. You can take that term 'wake' any way—"

Ramona interrupted. "What are you talking about, Glen?"

He smiled engagingly. "Sorry. That was a little confusing,

wasn't it? I'll start at the beginning."

Angela saw her fingertips white on the glass. She could feel Glen watching her.

"Thomas Dawn," he began, "came to me this morning. He came in the role of spokesman for all the men. Why? Not because he's a union official, which he isn't. He came because he's supposed to be my brother-in-law. Now I might negotiate through a union, if I thought their demands were reasonable, but I will not negotiate with some nonentity, just because he claims a tie of kinship."

He hates me, she thought, and remembered the dry ice. Probably it really happened. Then why had he taken it away?

Ramona was asking, "What did they want?"

"What do they always want?" He smiled again. It ended in a rueful shrug. "More money. What else? Shorter hours. Hell, the work's almost finished, and they want shorter hours so they can get more overtime."

"I suppose they thought you'd give in to them," Ramona said, glancing uncomfortably at Angela, "just to get it done. They know how much it means to you."

"To me!" Glen exclaimed. "It's the water system. New York City's eight million."

His response gave Angela a moment of smug pleasure. He was still unwilling to admit that it had become a personal thing.

But the pleasure died away and left her afraid. *He hates me. He tried to kill me.*

Even her sickness . . .

She heard Ramona ask, "So you fired this man. Does that end it?"

And Glen: "Not at all. You see, there are the unions. That's what Flora and I are working on now."

He hates me.

Their faces wavered, disconnected blobs. The blobs began to move and she saw that they were getting up from the table. She got up, too, but could not feel herself standing.

She started up the stairs. Someone called to her. They were going into the living room to have their coffee. It would be more comfortable for her there, they said. She had not drunk coffee in months. It made her sick.

Before closing the suite door, she waited to see if anyone had followed. No one had. The stairs were empty.

What did he expect her to do? Again she remembered the ice bucket. Maybe he only took it away because all the ice had evaporated and she was still alive.

But then he had showed her the bottle that next evening. They had drunk out of it together. Maybe he only wanted to frighten her, to warn her. Maybe he wanted to drive her away.

Dazed, she began to fold some of her clothes, and the children's clothes. The pink corduroy overalls Donna had worn the last time they visited the dam.

She paused. He would never let her take the children. She had planned to take them without asking him, but he would fight to get them back, and he would win. Then two more little Glens would grow up in Villa Fabiani.

They must not be left behind, but she did not know how to get them out. At that moment they were in Stella's apartment, probably asleep.

She did not know how to do any of this. She needed help. With her dizzy spells, she had been afraid to drive the car. Glen had ordered it put on blocks, and the battery removed. Furthermore, she could not expect help from Glen's family. Even Stella and Albert were his.

She picked up the telephone and dialed Tom's number.

It was Betty who answered. When she heard Angela's voice, her own rose shrilly.

"Do you know what he did to your brother, Angela Dawn? Angela *Fabian*? I never heard of anybody being fired for—"

"Wait, Betty, not now. I need Tom. I'm scared. Get Tom for me, *please*."

There was startled silence, and after a moment, voices in the background. She hunched over the phone, seeing waves of blackness.

And then Tom. "Hi, Angela, what's up?"

"Tom, I know what happened. Never mind. Please come and get me out of here. Now. He hates me and I'm afraid to stay."

"He hates *you*?"

"I don't have time to talk about it. I have to get the children. Come up with your lights off and wait for me."

She hung up before he could ask more questions. By then, her legs were shaking and she could barely walk. She stuffed a few clothes into a shoulder bag. There was no time really to pack, and she could not carry much.

She slipped down the stairway and through the empty, darkened dining room. Voices came faintly from some distance away. Thank God they were still in the living room. And Stella?

In the kitchen. Angela could hear her loading the dishwasher. She could not get into Stella's suite without going through the kitchen, unless she went around outside, and the back door might be locked.

Then she heard the children. They, too, were in the kitchen. Stella allowed them to stay up late and sleep until noon. It was probably easier for her. Angela's annoyance gave way to relief that they were accessible. At least she

177

would not have to wake them. But how to get them out from under Stella's nose?

She listened, dodging back behind the china cabinets when footsteps came closer. At any moment, the swinging door would open. What if the light went on?

The steps moved away. But Stella was still there, in the kitchen. And Tom would be coming. How long would he wait?

Then, thank God, the buzzer. A summons from Ramona.

Stella had a heavy walk. Angela heard it enter the passageway and grow fainter. Quickly she slipped into the kitchen.

"Mom—!" Michael began. She put her finger to her lips, scooped up Donna, took Michael by the arm and led them to the door. There was no time even for coats.

As she opened the door, Albert emerged from his room. He sized them up and took a step toward them. She plunged through the door, dragging Michael, who protested loudly.

The night was bitter and windy and Tom was not there. She forgot her sickness, forgot that the children had no coats as she began to run—through the parking area, past the garage, toward the driveway.

In front of the house, a car waited. She stumbled, her heart pounding. She had forgotten to tell him to meet her at the back. He slid toward them, his lights dark, and opened a door. She dived in beside him with both the children and her bulky shoulder bag.

Tom said, "You're being kind of melodramatic, aren't you?"

"I don't know." A wave of nausea washed over her. She began to shiver. "I just don't know what might happen. He'd never let me take the kids."

Tom turned on his lights and sped down the hill. They

had reached the foot and were on the highway when she caught a flash of headlights through the trees. Another car shot out of the Fabian driveway.

She gasped in alarm. But the car rushed past them, its taillights disappearing in the direction of Kaaterskill. Glen, with that girl, going back to the office.

Did that mean that Albert hadn't said anything? He was slow at times. Or perhaps Glen had not recognized the car. It was perfect timing. If they had still been on the driveway, he might have tried to stop them. Likewise if they had already turned in at Florence's house, which they did a moment later. But on the public road they were only an anonymous vehicle.

By then, she had the children wrapped in their jackets. Michael had stopped being outraged and decided they were having fun. Donna echoed everything that Michael said or felt.

Florence came from the kitchen, staring with her mouth open as all four entered the house. Angela sagged onto the sofa and closed her eyes. She heard Tom speaking. Florence took the children and put them to bed in Tom's old room, then returned for an explanation.

Angela did not know how to explain. There was the champagne bottle and the dry ice, but that was insubstantial. It might even have been a mere thoughtless accident, but she doubted it.

"All I know is," she said to Tom, "when he came home tonight with a girl and told us what happened between you and him, I could tell he hated me. I'm afraid of him. There are reasons—but I can't talk about it."

"Yeah, the guy's gotten fanatical." Tom nodded wisely. "But why'd you have to sneak off like that? If he hates you, wouldn't he want to see you go?"

"I'm not sure what he wants. But it was the children. He'd never—he'll want them back. And you know how he is."

"For God's sake, if you're trying to hide," said Tom, "why'd you come here?"

"Where else, in the middle of the night? And it wouldn't matter where I went, he could always find me. I'm going to call him tomorrow anyway and make it official. I just wanted to get the children away."

"All that secrecy, and you're going to *call* him?"

"I told you, it was to get the children out."

"Then why didn't you bring them yourself in the morning, like you were coming for a visit? Wouldn't that be easier?"

"Because I hardly ever *see* the kids. And Glen put my car on blocks. He said it was to save the tires. I know it was so I couldn't take the children. You don't understand what's been happening. The thing today—it was sort of a crisis. It made me realize—more dry ice—" She pressed a pillow to her face and started to cry.

The next morning, after an hour of misgivings and dread, she telephoned Glen at his office.

Flora Bernhofer took the call. Undoubtedly she knew of Angela's flight and probably thought it was because of her. An amused lilt touched her voice. It was a long time before Glen came onto the telephone.

His laughter crackled over the wire. "Do you know what you're doing, Angela dear? You're showing your class. After all those years at my house, it finally comes out."

"What does?" Of all possible reactions, she had not expected anything like this.

"Your class," he repeated. "You're identifying with that brother of yours, the working class. From overalls to overalls in one generation."

"Glen, that's not the reason." She had almost forgotten about Tom.

"You can do what you like with yourself, dear, but I'll expect the children home by tonight."

Even knowing this would happen, she felt something clutch at her throat when he said it.

"No, Glen, they're staying with me."

"I don't intend to argue about it. They are not staying with you." He hung up the phone.

She folded over, her heart chugging painfully. She had hoped, only hoped, he would not want the children. Now what?

She tried to think of a father's love. But that was gone. He did not love anyone, if he ever had. He only wanted them for his ego, his dynasty. And they would be molded like him.

Somehow, they would have to be taken out of his reach. But how?

She did not really have any friends, at least no one close enough whom she could trust. No one but Tom. She picked up the phone again and called him, almost glad, for the moment, that he had lost his job and was available.

Tom pondered the situation. "I could keep them here."

"That would be the second place he'd look," she said. "There's nowhere I can take them. He's got the resources to trace us wherever we go."

"Don't give up, Angela. We'll think of something."

"We have to think of something *now*. But there's no place. Nobody. It would have to be somewhere like New York, so big and crowded we'd never be found. But I don't know anybody there."

After a lengthy pause, which she dared not interrupt, Tom said, "Leave it to me. We'll work out something for the time being, and meanwhile, get yourself a lawyer. And

181

look, Angela, adults can be traced easier than kids. You have a Social Security number, things like that. It might be better if the kids go without you."

"*Without me?*"

"I really think it's better. And even better if you yourself don't know where they are. Then there's no way he can get it from you. But it's just for a while, till we get this straightened out, okay?"

It was not okay. He could not take them from her.

But if he didn't, Glen would get them. Not knowing what else to do, she agreed.

Half an hour later, Tom came in his car and took the children. They had hardly any clothes or possessions with them, but that, under the circumstances, seemed unimportant. She gave him all the money she had, to buy whatever they most needed and to pay for their keep until she could find a job.

She stood outside and watched him drive away. She saw their faces in the window. No one had any idea how long it would be, and there was no way of explaining to them, in terms they could understand, what was happening.

She went back into the house, her head throbbing, and sat down on the couch. Again she asked herself—what now? She needed some income, but was too sick to work. Although oddly enough, after surviving the crises of that morning, she felt stronger than she would have expected. Perhaps simply getting away from the Fabians had made a difference.

She would have to try. But her only work experience had been the job at the Fabian office. She would need their references.

Maybe not. She could try to explain. But there was the chance that, if he chose, Glen could have her blacklisted so that no one in the whole area would hire her. And if she

182

went somewhere else, her living expenses would be higher. Besides, she hadn't the strength to go out on her own.

She rested all day until Florence came home, bringing a dinner of frozen manicotti.

While they ate, Angela asked, "Do you think I could get a job at Villa Castelli? At least the Fabians don't own that."

"You shouldn't even think about a job," replied Florence. "How will you stay on your feet?"

"I'm better already. There's nothing like a shot of independence. I wonder if Tom's back yet."

She did not want to call, for fear of getting Betty on the phone.

"Now that you've left Glen," Florence said reasonably, "she shouldn't hold you responsible."

"She shouldn't anyway. I had nothing to do with it, but I can understand. What happened, exactly? Do you know?"

As far as Florence could tell, Tom had not even protested the firing. And afterward, Glen had reached an agreement with the other men and granted them, not shorter hours, but higher overtime pay.

"Higher!" exclaimed Angela. "How can he afford it? I just don't understand this."

"You and me both. I never did understand the business mind, anyhow. But why shouldn't they get their share, if Old Moneybags wants to throw it around?" Florence looked pleased, until she remembered that Tom was no longer in on the bonanza.

Recalling a long-ago remark of Glen's, Angela said, "Maybe it has something to do with politics. Maybe he has to get it done before somebody's term is up, or something. But what about the other men? Don't they care what happens to Tom? After all, he lost his job speaking for all of them. Aren't they going to do anything?"

"I thought so, but I guess they're not," said Florence.

183

"Moneybags must have bought them off with that higher pay."

"What's Tom going to do? Can he find another job?"

"Probably not around here. Not for a while, anyway. Betty's going back to work for now. They'll have unemployment, but it's not much."

"Where's she working?"

"She went down to La Suisse as soon as she heard about Tom, and got her old job back. She'll be working evenings instead of lunch. The tips are better at dinner, she says."

That night Angela lay restlessly in bed, while a late March wind whistled past the house. It was a horrible, lonely sound. She turned on a light. The night was dragging and she wanted something to read, but all her books were at Villa Fabiani. All except one. On the otherwise empty shelf in her room she saw the book Glen had given her, *The Language of Cheirosophy*, which she had left at her grandmother's. Tom must have brought it here for her to pick up.

At least it would help to pass the time. She sat in bed and idly turned the pages, stopping when she came to a photograph of something that looked like a rubber glove standing on a pedestal. A cast of the hand of Napoleon, the caption said. It took her back to the old palmistry book Lydia had given her, in which she first read about the Jupiter finger. Mrs. Hunt had mentioned the Sign of the Tyrant, an abnormally long index finger, and said Napoleon's was like that.

Sleet began to rattle against the window. She went on turning the pages. She came to a chapter on the Line of the Head and glanced over it, skimming, until a word or two caught her eye.

In the class of murderer for gain, the most prominent mark is the line of head, which will be heavily defined and in an abnormal position, rising upward toward Mercury.

184

On meeting the line of heart, it will swallow it up, thus smothering any instinct toward love and charity. The thumb in this case is stiff, the whole hand is hard and grasping, for this is a person who will stop at nothing to satisfy his covetous desires.

For a long time she stared at the paragraph. In her mind, she saw Glen's hand.

She had never thought of his thumb as stiff, nor his hand as particularly grasping, although it was certainly not a soft hand. And the Glen she once knew had had some instincts toward love and charity. At least toward love. But for some reason the paragraph struck her, and she could not understand why. It was really only his Head Line that matched the description in the book.

Much later, as she lay in the dark, nearly asleep, she heard a faint whisper: *The mark of the murderer on his hand.*

She was suddenly wide awake. It had been a whisper in her own mind, but she thought what it said was true.

She remembered the workmen who had died at the dam. Murdered by speed and impatience.

She remembered Whitman. Murdered by scandal and despair. By false witness?

She remembered Bruno. Murdered?

It was possible. She had wondered about the accident, and Ramona had not liked her questions. Glen had asked the police to inspect the car, but that might have been only a coverup, a diversion.

And there was the dry ice.

Her thoughts churned, unresolved. *The mark of the murderer on his hand.* A person could not be convicted, even figuratively, because of a mark on his hand.

But it fit. It did fit. Those deaths . . .

185

21

Within a few days of her departure from Villa Fabiani, Angela's health began to improve. At first she attributed it to simple relief. But her troubles were far from over, and her improvement was so sure and rapid that she concluded it must have had another cause.

Something, or someone, had been making her sick. It was not the first time she had thought it, but the first time she actually believed it. She recognized the possibility that it might have been accidental, something to which only she had been exposed. Or a combination of things.

But maybe it was not accidental.

Who was it? she wondered. Glen? He was scarcely ever there. The gentle, chilly, and somewhat ineffectual Ramona? Perhaps the faithful Stella. Or all of them. But if it were true, she thought the doctors should have been able to find something in her bloodstream. She visited a third, who only shook his head and clearly did not believe her. She even began to doubt herself. Perhaps it was a virus after all.

Whatever the cause of her illness, now that it had nearly gone, she could begin to think seriously about working. She needed a job within walking distance, for she had no car of her own. The closest possibility was La Suisse Restaurant.

Betty, believing that she had left Glen out of loyalty to Tom, was only too glad to introduce her to the manager. With the approach of the resort season, he never had enough local help, and hired Angela immediately.

The restaurant opened at eleven o'clock for lunch and stopped serving dinner at nine. Most of the waitresses worked either the lunch or dinner shift. Because she was starting life again with nearly nothing, and required money for the children as well as herself, Angela took both shifts. In the middle of the afternoon she would have some free time, but not enough to go home. They told her, even without knowing she had been sick, that she would probably drop dead from exhaustion. That was all right, too. At least she would be too busy to think.

Too busy to think of the phone call from Glen on the afternoon before she was to begin work.

She had expected it—sometime—but it startled and frightened her to hear his voice.

"The children," he said, with no preliminaries. "Angela, I was quite serious about that."

"Yes, Glen, I understand, but you see—they're not here. I don't know where they are, and that's the honest truth. But you can be sure they're perfectly safe."

"How do you know that," he asked, "if you don't know where they are?"

"I know it—from a very responsible person."

"All right, let's stop playing games. Who has the kids?"

"I told you, I have no idea."

"I find that hard to believe, but it's possible. In which case, you must have an intermediary. Who is it? Your brother?"

She was glad he couldn't see her. She would have betrayed everything. Rallying, she said, "I have other friends. I grew up in this town, remember?"

"I told you to stop playing games."

She should have thought of this. Tom should have, too. Obviously she would need a connection of some kind.

"It's somebody I know in Albany," she invented. "A lawyer. That's as much as I'm going to tell you."

"Angela, I want those children. And I want them by tomorrow night."

It would give her some time to elaborate on the lawyer, to think of a name and address.

"I'll see what I can do, Glen."

Tomorrow night. She would be at work, and Florence would come home first. There was no telling what Glen might try. She called Tom to alert him.

"Don't worry about anything," he said. "I'll be over there tomorrow."

She could not stop herself from worrying. What could Tom do against Glen? But he was there as he had promised, to receive Glen's second phone call.

"The children aren't here," was Tom's answer. "Angela told you that. I really don't know where they are, and neither does she."

Glen threatened a lawsuit and gave another deadline: the following night. Tom waited again, ready for a showdown, but Glen did not call. Later Tom heard that there had been a minor emergency at the dam. It must have been more than minor, he thought, as the days went by and they heard no more from Glen.

The dam was a favorite topic among the employees at La Suisse. Angela found herself in closer touch with it there than she had been at Villa Fabiani. The work was nearly finished, she learned. The reservoir was rising faster than anyone had expected.

Betty confided one afternoon as they set their tables, "I'm really glad it happened, about Tom getting fired. I was scared. They were putting up that thing so fast it wasn't safe. It's a miracle there were only two killed."

Then she recollected Angela's connection with the dam. Her dark eyes flashed a look that was both apologetic and defiant.

"I wouldn't know," Angela said. "I don't know anything about building a dam. But if you're glad, then I am, too."

"I wonder if you're going to get divorced—" Betty seized her arm. "Angela, did you see who just walked into the bar?"

The bar, a separate room beyond an archway, was dimly lit. It took Angela a moment to figure out who Betty meant.

"David Bennett!"

"I haven't seen him in here before," Betty said.

"I haven't seen him at all since December."

From time to time as she worked, Angela glanced into the bar, where David sat with a friend. She wanted to tell him what had happened to her, and to hear about Ecuador. After a while he noticed her, grinned and waved. He did not seem to wonder what she was doing there.

He waved again as he left, but he never returned. A month later they learned he had taken a job as a crop-duster pilot, spraying the apple orchards south of the Catskills.

Although her work was strenuous, Angela's health had returned to normal, and she could handle it. The miraculous and spontaneous improvement again made her suspicious as to the cause of her illness. She found it hard to believe they would go so far as to hurt her deliberately.

But if it were true, it frightened her to think what Glen might do to get the children back. She hired a lawyer to help her legitimize her situation and to handle the custody fight when it came.

In dread, she waited for Glen to make his next move. His very silence kept her nerves on edge. She supposed it was possible that he was too engrossed in the dam to put his mind on anything else. It was equally possible that he was coiling up for a big strike.

By June the dam was finished.

Now, she thought. Now he would come after her with all his artillery.

Still she heard nothing. He could not have given up, or forgotten. That was not like Glen.

The dam—finished. She could scarcely believe it, after so much time. It had dominated their lives, perhaps reached even farther than that. She did not know whether the dam had changed Glen, or whether the change in Glen had brought about the dam.

"Have you seen it?" Florence asked her. "You have a day off. Take my car. I can get a ride with somebody. You really should see it. After all, you had a lot to do with it."

More than you know, Angela thought.

She started out in the middle of the morning, driving over the winding road that held so many memories. Memories of happy times with Glen and the children, and memories of that tragic day when the workmen were killed. After nearly an hour she arrived at the hill where Glen had first told her about the dam.

This time she looked down on a vast sheet of water. No longer, even in her imagination, could she see the church spire, and the farms and fields. Instead she saw the sky reflected. And between the ridge where she stood, and the next one, there rose a majestic giant of ivory-colored concrete that seemed to glow in the sunlight.

Below its face, where the rocky riverbed of the Cat now ran almost dry, the old field office remained. A small crew still worked there, cleaning up the mess of construction and maintaining the dam.

As she walked back to her car, reluctantly impressed, she

reminded herself that Glen had not done it alone. It had been all of them together, the engineers, designers, the workmen, even the office people.

She had just opened the door when the sound of another car made her turn around.

The gray Mercedes. It was the only kind he ever owned. It drew up behind her own car and stopped.

Glen was not alone. Next to him, in the passenger seat, sat an immaculate young man in a light blue suit.

Glen got out of the car and came toward her.

"Well, Angela, it's been quite a while. And what brings you out into the fresh air from the fetid kitchen at La Suisse?"

She watched him, dreading, only a part of her remembering that she had once loved him. She had been stupid to come here.

"It's my day off," she answered. "I heard the dam was finished and I wanted to see it."

"Oh?"

It took her a moment to realize that he must have thought she was on her way to visit the children.

He seemed to regret having betrayed himself. Fully recovered, he said, "Do be our guest. Presumably the dam belongs to the people. And in the meantime, meet my friend Stanley Morales." He gestured toward his passenger, who was getting out of the car. "Stan, the estranged wife."

Stanley Morales. One of the men who had testified against Whitman.

Morales gave her a gleaming smile and held out his hand.

"That's right, Angela, shake hands," Glen advised. "You can always say you were one of the first. The next time you meet Stanley, maybe at the restaurant or someplace, he'll be a congressman. That's not a bad beginning, is it? I expect you to vote for Stanley in November."

191

"Provided I get the nomination." Stanley's grin was confident.

"You'll get it," said Glen.

Reaching out, he had told her once. *Maybe there's something more than construction and contracting.*

"So you've gone into politics," she said. "I'm surprised you found the time."

"Always time for a friend." Glen winked at his companion.

"What's your field," she asked Morales, "besides politics?"

"I'm a lawyer," he replied, still smiling.

"I suppose you're representing Glen's interests?"

"No, I'd be more inclined to say Glen's representing my interests." He laughed heartily.

What, then, she wondered, had he to do with Whitman Fabian, that he had been in a position to make a complaint against him for improper advances? But she supposed a way could always be found. And this was the payoff. Glen would back his campaign and pull strings for him. Glen could do it, because he had friends. The big men, the influential ones. The men who had made Glen what he was.

She turned the key in her ignition. "It was nice meeting you, Mr. Morales."

"My pleasure entirely."

With a last look at the dam, she turned her car around and headed back over the mountains. She half expected Glen to stop her. Perhaps he had changed his mind about the children—but she was sure he hadn't. He was only waiting for a better time and place.

She had not wished Morales luck in his campaign. He did not need luck. And she still saw Whitman lying in his own blood on the basement floor.

How, she wondered, had Glen managed all this? She knew he could not have done it, couldn't do what he was doing, without help. She knew he had help, but did not

192

know who they were. Powerful people, who remained in the background. People who would expect favors, or perhaps had already been granted them. Glen had moved into a different world. A worldly world where deals were made, and where dirty money changed hands.

She drove back to Burley's Falls in the high sunlight of the June afternoon. The mountains, the forests, all appeared pure and clean and fine. Life itself had once seemed that way. She ought, perhaps, to have known better.

They had had something, she and Glen, when they began. It was the dam that had changed him.

The prophecy. And Marcia's death.

But he must have had it in him anyway, she thought. The prophecy only brought it out.

Betty and Glen—two such different people, but both had believed. How many others were there? she wondered again on a steamy afternoon in July.

It was the slow time of day, between lunch and dinner. Betty had arrived and they were sitting at a corner table drinking iced coffee before the evening rush began. A radio in the kitchen played music and periodically rattled off the local news. It was a hot and lazy day, even in the air-cooled restaurant.

The kitchen door burst open. Fat Irma Brown, one of the chef's helpers, her hands dusty with flour, rushed over to their table, panting heavily.

"Girls, did you hear the news? Just now, on the radio. You know that fellow you went to school with? The one who flew the plane? He got killed."

Angela stared at her through a dark haze. Betty's long spoon clattered to the floor.

Betty said it for both of them. "David—Bennett?"

"That's it. That's the one." Irma was in her glory, the

193

first to bring the news. "He crashed. His plane. It knocked into some trees and hit the ground. They fly low, you know, those crop-dusters."

"It's not true!" Angela cried.

"They do," insisted Irma.

"David." Betty started to cry. Irma patted her shoulder, floury hands and all, now sorry that she had so relished telling them.

"Angela, I want to go home," Betty wept.

"They'll never let you."

"But I'm sick."

"So am I."

After a few moments, Betty managed to control herself. Irma stood back to see whether they would make it, then drifted away to the kitchen, the excitement gone from her face.

"I don't know," Betty said. "Somehow it seems worse than Marcia. I mean, after all that time in the jungle, with those air currents—and now a silly tree."

Angela agreed. "It's much worse than Marcia. I really liked David. When Marcia died, at least for me it was just sort of horrifying."

"Maybe it isn't really true."

"She heard it on the radio."

"Maybe he's not—dead."

But he was. They heard it confirmed on a later broadcast.

On the way home that night they paid a sympathy visit to the Bennetts. George told them he couldn't believe it; the day had been still, with good visibility and no wind. "David musta just been too sure of himself," he said. He added that Zinnia was on her way up from New York, and that David had been taken to Hartmann's Funeral Home in Kaaterskill.

Two days later Angela borrowed her mother's car, and in the early morning, drove to Kaaterskill.

The funeral home was not expecting visitors quite so early. She waited while they prepared the casket, and then was led into the room where he lay, a calm, unreal figure. All traces of the crash had been skillfully covered.

"Could I be alone for just a minute?" she asked. Mr. Hartmann was already leaving the room.

She moved closer to the body. Death was not new to her, but still it was strange and rather terrifying. She reminded herself that this was David, her friend.

Very gently she lifted his left hand where she had seen the Square of Protection—the mark he believed would carry him safely through any danger. The mark which, if palmistry were to be taken seriously, should have helped him through those dangerous flights in the jungle and protected him from the treetops he skimmed on his last day.

For a long time she contemplated his palm, recalling the lines, the markings, from that Halloween ball nearly six years before. But one was gone, if it had ever been there. She had been so sure, and yet there was not even a hint of it. The Square of Protection had vanished.

22

She told no one of her visit to David, but she thought about it all day. She wondered if he had really believed her. Or maybe she only caused him to start thinking, and he did what he wanted to do anyway. It was luck and skill that had kept him alive in the jungle, and bad luck or misjudgment that had finally killed him. That was all it was.

But late at night, after getting into bed, she looked through her cheirosophy book. The only thing she found was an obscure observation that "the lines can change." There was no reference anywhere to the Square of Protection.

The next morning she attended the funeral with Betty and Tom. Zinnia was there, her mascara smudged with crying. She gave Angela a perfunctory hug and they spoke briefly, recalling David. That afternoon, Zinnia went back to New York. She did not seem at all interested in Katie June, who was by then a well-behaved and very pretty four-year-old. It made Angela miss her own children all the more.

The rains continued to fall and Glen's reservoir to fill. Glen had everything he wanted, she noted bitterly, while David had lost even his life. There was no justice in the universe.

Glen did not have quite all he wanted. He did not have the children. But now that the dam was finished, he would be able to give his full attention to getting them back. And when a custody fight arose, he would have no trouble demonstrating how much he could do for them, while Angela, a working mother, could not even give them her own time.

"Why don't you look for an office job?" Florence suggested. "That's professional, anyway. It might help."

"There wouldn't be any office jobs except in Kaaterskill," Angela replied, "and I don't have a car. And if I take a bus and have to work late . . ."

Florence beamed beneficently. "You can have my car. For keeps. I go crazy every time it rains and the thing won't start, so I decided to get a new one. I already picked it out."

With the promise of a car, on her next day off Angela went to Kaaterskill and applied for several jobs. She knew she had been a good secretary, but the employers seemed oddly evasive. They were probably afraid to take a chance on her. Glen was too powerful.

And so she remained at La Suisse, and in the end, was glad she did. It was at La Suisse, one cool night in August, that she first caught sight of a dark, handsome stranger.

But he was not a stranger. She noticed him because he looked familiar.

It couldn't be, she thought. He was so different. And yet she knew him.

"Ross!"

He saw her at the same moment and hurried over to help lift the heavy tray down from her shoulder. Their hands touched, bringing back sudden memories of long ago.

"What are you doing here?" he asked. "Like this?"

"What does it look as if I'm doing? Ross, are you alone? Why don't you sit at my table?"

He took the one she pointed out, a table for two next to the wall.

"It's great to see you, Angela, but what is this? What happened? I thought you had it made."

"Everything happened," she said. "It's a long story. About the dam, mostly. And him. I had to get away."

He did not seem surprised. "Are you making it legal? I did."

"So I heard. I even saw Zinnia this summer. She came for David's funeral. You heard about David?"

Ross had heard. His family still lived in Burley's Falls, and he was not out of touch.

The restaurant was busy that evening, but as often as she could, she lingered by his table.

"What have you been doing all this time?" she asked. "They said you were in New York."

"Yeah, I was. No particular reason at first, except I have relatives there. When I got settled, I had some time to think, so I decided to go back to school."

"That's wonderful. Have you finished?"

"I got an engineering degree. I have a job that starts in September, and I'll be going on for my master's."

"That's a lot of work."

"It's worth it."

Ross Giordano, always aimless and angry. She wondered what had changed him. Was it the responsibilities of that brief marriage?

When she passed his table again, she asked, "What made you leave Burley's Falls? I mean, so suddenly."

"It's because of something that happened," he said. "I'll tell you later."

She expected that he, like David, would walk away and not return. But long after the tables were cleared and reset for lunch, and she left the restaurant, she found him waiting in his car, listening to a stereo tape.

"How about a ride home?" he asked.

"Oh, thanks. Tom usually picks up Betty and me, but—"

"Then we'll wait for Betty."

She went inside to notify Betty and call Tom. When she returned to Ross, he had switched off the tape. He sat watching her, saying nothing.

"You were going to tell me why you left town," she reminded him. "I know there was some trouble around that time. I was having it, too."

"Yeah," he breathed, meeting her eyes. "Yeah, it was Zinnia, but it wasn't Glen that particular time. There were a lot more than Glen. And you had something to do with what happened. That's why I wanted to tell you."

"*I* did?"

"Yes. Remember that time you were telling my fortune?"

"Oh, God, that damned Halloween dance. Do you realize, my whole life—"

He cut her short. "Not the dance, another time. At Sal's, I think. Remember, you came in and looked at my hand, and you said I should watch my temper? You said if I didn't, something bad would happen."

She nodded.

"Well," he continued, "I don't know how you knew, but I remembered it just in time. It was in the summer. I guess you know which one. The first summer we were both married, and my daughter was born. After the baby came, I lost my job, and Zinnia went back to work for Glen."

"How can I forget?"

"Zinnia—well, she started playing around." He shifted nervously, turning slightly away from her. "At first I couldn't prove anything, but I was pretty sure. Then one day I came home when she didn't expect me. I found her with a— some creep. I didn't know him. I just walked in and there they were. I felt this big rush of blood in my head. I didn't have any thoughts. Only the feeling that I had to do something. I even picked up a—I don't know, a brick. I can still see him cowering. And then I remembered what you said. And I knew that was it. That was what you meant."

The only sound was the distant slam of a car door and voices across the parking lot.

"It caught me," he said after a moment, "just like that. As if something exploded in my head. Like stars, you know, when you get hit. Then it was dark and quiet. I put down the brick—we used it for a doorstop—and just walked out. I kept on walking for a couple of hours, and then I went back and packed my clothes and told Zinnia I was leaving. And I went to New York."

"Ross . . ." She fumbled for words, wanting him to know that in all those years, this was the first good thing to come from her fortune-telling.

He did not wait for her. "So I want to say thanks," he added. "But I always wondered, how could you tell? What was it you saw?"

"It was a cross. Right at the end of your Fate Line. They call it the Mark of the Scaffold. It's—"

She lifted his hand. He took a flashlight from the glove compartment and shone it on his palm.

"I don't see it," she said in bewilderment. "I'm sure it was there."

They both searched for the mark, but could not find it.

Angela said, "I don't believe this."

"Why not? You're a living thing. The rest of your body changes. Can't the hand change, too?"

"Yes, it can. I suppose if you really want to believe in

this stuff, then that was the time it referred to. That could have been your destiny. You could have killed them, but you didn't. You changed your own destiny, and then your hand changed, too."

"You believe that?" he asked.

"No, I said *if* you want to believe it, you could interpret it that way. But I don't know. I still can't swallow all those things."

And yet Ross had, at least in that moment, and it had changed his life. What he had done was right, but for a man of his temperament, and in those circumstances, it had taken courage and effort. Maybe, she thought, in the end, that was what it was all about. Maybe it only served to direct what was already in the unconscious mind.

And that was true, too, in the case of Glen.

Ross said, with some embarrassment, "I can't swallow it, either."

"That's what people say, but I don't know." She told him what she had been thinking, about himself, and Glen.

She told about David, too, and Betty. And even Marcia, adding, "Marcia never knew her prediction, so that can't have had anything to do with it. And David—I still don't understand about David. His mark disappeared, like yours. But why?"

"It depends, I guess, on whether you want to look at it anatomically or—some other way."

"Cheirosophically. Well, I wouldn't know the answer in either case. Ross, I just remembered something. Didn't I tell you that, according to your hand, you ought to study law?"

He laughed softly. "I held my temper when I should have. Isn't that enough?"

"But why engineering?"

"I like it. All phases of it. In fact, I wish I could have

201

been here when they were building the dam. Tomorrow I'm going up to see it."

Betty came out of the restaurant, apologizing for having made them wait.

"Perfectly all right," said Ross. "We had an interesting talk."

As they left the parking lot, drops of rain spattered the windshield. Angela remembered her grandmother down the mountain and was almost glad the Cat had been dammed. If it were running as it once had, with the addition of all the rain, she might have been washed away.

Ross eased his car over the rutted driveway, which had only grown worse with constant rain, and stopped beside the porch. Angela got out, wondering whether she would see him again.

"Good night, both of you." And to Ross: "I hope you like the dam. Let me know if it's spilling over yet."

She stood on the porch, hearing the rain all around her, and thought of the reservoir rising. She thought of the dam, holding back all those tons of water. No wonder that, to Glen, it had been a symbol of power.

23

The next afternoon, Ross stopped again at La Suisse. He took the same table and ordered black coffee and a slice of apple pie.

Angela asked, "Did you see the dam? How did you like it?"

"Real nice." His voice lacked enthusiasm. "I mean, it's nice from an esthetic point of view. Whoever designed it did a good job. But—"

"But what? What's wrong with it?"

"Nothing's wrong with the planning, as far as I can see. It even," he went on, evading her, "goes nicely with its setting. There's good harmony there. It seems to fit in naturally."

"Then what didn't you like?"

"It's not a matter of what I like. I'm not sure the thing is structurally sound."

She stared at him. "What are you talking about?"

"What could be plainer? Maybe you don't want to know what I'm talking about. Your husband cut corners, Angela. He was in a big hurry to get it finished."

"Well, I know that, but—*structurally*? I wouldn't have thought he. . . . Anyway, it's going to be all right, isn't it?"

"Probably. But it will need a lot of repair work over the years, for which I suppose Glen will get the contracts. And it might not last as long as a well-built dam."

"But, if it doesn't last, what happens?"

"Let's just hope somebody has the good sense to notice it isn't lasting and drain the reservoir before the whole thing goes. They'd have done better to build an earth dam. That'd be stronger. A gravity dam depends on its own weight for strength, and I don't think they put enough into it. That's only my opinion. I'm no expert."

"Glen doesn't decide on the type of dam," she said.

"I know. But if they planned a gravity dam, it should have been built stronger."

"Wouldn't he have to follow the specifications?"

"Yes, he would, except contractors have all sorts of ways of doing those things."

"Well, anyway," she was beginning to feel almost defensive, "don't you think this one looks nice?"

"Nothing wrong with an earth dam. It's cheaper to build, too, as long as you have plenty of earth. All the newer ones around here are earth."

He went on to talk of "Cyclopean concrete blocks," which she assumed was what the older dams were made of. She did not understand all he said, but wondered how right he was. Glen was an engineer and he worked with engineers. The planning must have been expert. But as Ross said, a builder could cut corners. He could bend the rules, use shoddy materials, and even cheat. She found it hard to believe that Glen would have cheated on the dam itself. He loved it too much.

She remembered the dispute at the time of Bruno's death, when the engineers had recommended a different type of dam. That was when all the trouble began. Still, it must have been smoothed out. The entire project involved the

204

use of public funds and therefore the supervision of public officials. Glen could not have cheated on that.

Could he?

Ross seemed transfixed by the dam. He went to look at it nearly every day, and almost as often, would visit the restaurant, or call Angela at home, to tell her he had been there. And yet he was always careful not to be seen alone with her, for fear it would give Glen some legal leverage to gain custody of the children.

One afternoon, over his usual coffee at La Suisse, she asked him, "Why does the dam fascinate you so much? There are plenty of others you could study. All kinds of dams. Earth fill, gravity. Cyclopean concrete blocks."

"I've seen them all," he told her. "After I looked at Glen's, I got interested. I've been driving around the area, even to the Croton and Kensico dams. But Glen's—it's really the most interesting. You see, the others are soundly built."

It continued to rain more than usual during the summer. The reservoir grew still larger, creeping up the sides of the hills that encircled it. She looked forward to seeing it full, so full that water would flow over the spillway. Ross found the prospect somewhat less exciting.

"That's a lot of weight," he said, "and the dam is so new. It should have some time to season and harden."

On Labor Day afternoon, he stopped at the restaurant to say good-bye to her. He was returning to New York to begin his job, and soon his graduate studies.

"I'll be back," he promised, "to see my daughter, and check on the dam."

"Why do you have to check?" she asked.

"I want to know how it holds up against all that water."

She felt a stab of alarm. "Isn't it supposed to hold up against all the water? Isn't that what it's for?"

205

"Yes, Angela, that is what it's for. We'll have to wait and see. As I said—"

"But you said it would hold. You did!"

"I said probably, and it probably will." He took her hand and held it in both of his. "Don't worry. It'll be okay. Glen wouldn't be so stupid. Anyhow, I'll see you."

Later that month he returned for a weekend. He and Katie June went to look at the dam, and then he took her to the restaurant for ice cream. Angela had seen her from time to time in the village, a lovely little girl with brown doe eyes and Zinnia's dainty mouth.

"After I get my master's," Ross confided, "and things ease up a little, I'm going to take her to live with me. It's something to work for, isn't it? Should make it easier on the Bennetts, too."

In spite of his busy schedule, he made another trip north in October. Again he visited La Suisse with his daughter.

"It's fantastic," he told Angela, "the way that thing's filling up. I thought it would take a couple of years at least. That's one thing they did right, was figuring out the watershed."

A few days later, she looked up from a tableful of patrons to see Glen enter the restaurant. He was accompanied by Stanley Morales. As they passed through into the bar, Glen's eyes raked over her. She felt a chill of apprehension, especially as the bar had a separate entrance and he could have gone in that way. Perhaps he had wanted to see if she was there.

Half an hour later, Glen came back alone into the restaurant. By then it was the slack time in the middle of the afternoon. Only one of her tables was occupied. She stood against the wall and watched him approach.

He asked quietly, "Aren't you going to say hello, Angela?"

Her voice emerged tight and nervous. "How are you, Glen?"

"A more pertinent question might be how are *you*? I

gather you're feeling better than you were, say, last winter. It could be this is really the place for you. You weren't happy up at the villa, were you?"

"For a while I was, but I," she cleared her throat, "I guess you and I weren't meant for each other. I should have known that right from the beginning, when—"

She had been about to confront him with Zinnia, but she had no way to prove it. There was even the chance that she might have been wrong, except for what Ross had mentioned.

He ignored her and asked very pointedly how the children were doing.

Her heart began to beat faster. It was coming now, and she was not prepared to handle it.

"I haven't seen them," she said, "but they're all right. I do know that."

"And how do you know that?"

As she tried to form a reply, he folded his arms and sat back against an empty table.

"I wonder, Angela, if you're aware of how the law works. You might very well be considered an unfit mother, sending your children off with unknown people to some unknown place. If it's really true that you don't know where they are, then how can you assure me that they're all right?"

"They are all right." She tried to speak confidently. "I can guarantee it."

"Can you? Then I would like you to prove it. I would like to see those children. Next Sunday, up at the house. Is that understood? Or would you prefer to hear it from my lawyer?"

"I know how you feel, Glen. I miss them, too." She was suddenly sorry for him.

"Those children belong at Villa Fabiani," he said, "and I intend to raise them there. I'll be expecting them on Sunday. Otherwise we're going to have to take you to court, Angela."

Thoughts of habeas corpus flashed through her mind. And when it came to a legal custody suit, maybe he really could declare her unfit on the grounds he had stated. And that would be the end for her. The end of her children.

Yet he was their father. He had as much right to them as she did.

But no moral right, she thought as his face blurred before her. Not the kind of person he had become.

The people at her table signaled for her. "Excuse me," she said.

He fixed her with his eyes and repeated, "Sunday." Turning to go back to the bar, he glanced through the plate glass front of the restaurant. "Hell," she heard him mutter, and something about rain. She did not give it any thought. She was thinking of the children.

It did more than rain during the afternoon. It poured in torrents. At four o'clock, Betty arrived with water streaming from her raincoat. The ends of her hair, protruding from a plastic kerchief, were soaked.

"That *rain*," she exclaimed. "I got this wet just running from the house to the car, and the car into here."

Then Angela remembered what Glen had said.

"I wonder if something's wrong."

"Wrong with what?"

"The dam."

Betty's eyes opened wide. "You heard?"

"I didn't hear anything. Glen was just here and he started cursing when he saw the rain. I'd have thought he'd want rain. All the faster to fill up his reservoir."

Betty whispered excitedly, "Is that all you heard?"

"I wouldn't have thought anything about it," Angela replied, "except for Ross. He doesn't think the dam is sound."

With wet fingers, Betty took her arm and led her to a corner of the kitchen.

"Angela, Tom got a call from his old boss. From Glen's company. He wants a lot of men to be ready—when the rain stops—in case the dam needs repairing. That's all he said. He didn't say it does need repairing. He just said be ready."

"Oh, *Betty*!"

"How's that for news?"

"You mean Tom would go? After what Glen did to him?"

"He might. It's work, and—I guess he wants to see what's happening. Angela," her voice quivered, "I'm glad there's something wrong with the dam."

For the next three days and nights it rained. Angela watched the steady fall of water and the gray skies, but she was thinking of her children. Sunday . . . Sunday. . . . It was too soon. Tom had told her it would have to be her decision. Either way, she could lose them and probably would. Unless she simply took them and ran into hiding. But Glen would probably find her anywhere, and she would always be afraid.

24

Glen kept his composure as he toured the dam with Hank Haddonfield, the engineer, and Bernie O'Connor, foreman of the maintenance crew. They would never know how betrayed he felt.

"The ground's still shifting, huh, Hank?" O'Connor pointed out. It was less a question than a statement. Hank nodded, studying a crack that ran like a wavering pencil line from the base of the dam clear up the wall as far as they could see. A thin crack. To the eye, not much, but where it cracked, it was weak, and the earth would shift again. And there were others.

Even a mistress could betray you, Glen thought. Maybe especially a mistress, and the dam had been his. Everyone else thought so, and he admitted it. He had loved her.

"Too much water," Hank was saying. "Should have waited."

"Waited?" asked Glen, his voice strangely hoarse. "Held off the rain, you mean?"

They both looked at him, noticing the hoarseness. He added quickly, "If it's too much, let's start getting rid of it, O'Connor."

He would stay in control. And he would triumph.

O'Connor and his men opened the outlets beneath the

dam to drain countless gallons of water into the river. The process had to be a slow one, or the Cat would flood. Men worked in shifts around the clock, repairing the damage. At night, the entire area was floodlit so the work could go on. New cracks appeared. And it rained again.

To Betty, the dam had become a personal enemy.

"It's a failure, Angela, it's a failure! That whole dam—it's going to break."

"It won't break," Angela said. "They're draining out the water as fast as they can."

"How fast can you drain out all that water? Tom says the thing is just crumbling away. They can't keep up with it."

The state police, bracing themselves for the worst, planned a warning system. Four small villages lay along the banks of the Cat between the dam and Burley's Falls. Burley's Falls itself would not be in danger, because there the Cat ran through a deep ravine. But after Mile Gorge the river tumbled in falls and rapids down the Catskill escarpment to the valley, then past more farms and villages on its way to the Hudson.

Betty's excitement turned to dread.

"I don't really want anything to happen," she said. "It'd be horrible. All those people . . ."

"They're already planning how to get the people away," Angela reminded her.

"The farms. The animals."

"If they have enough warning . . ."

But it gave Angela something to think about. The next morning before work she drove down the mountain, in the car that was now hers, to her grandmother's house. Regardless of the changes everywhere else, Lydia Dawn and her chickens remained the same, and so did Lydia's sense of independence.

"Nothing's going to happen," she assured her granddaughter. "And I can't leave my chickens. Somebody has to stay here and feed them."

"Grandma," Angela begged, "I understand how you feel, but Tom says—"

"I know what Tom says. He's been here, too. He even offered to put the chickens in his garage." She chuckled at the very idea.

"It's not funny." Although, in a way, it was. "Tom should know what he's talking about. He's been working there, he's seen the dam. Look, Grandma, if that thing goes—"

"How am I going to round up all those chickens?" Lydia demanded. "There must be thirty, forty chickens. How am I going to get them all up the mountain? And what about my house? I can't leave my house. Somebody'll come along and rob me, God knows, they'll find something to take. You go on, Angela, I'll be all right. Whatever happened to that young man you married?"

Angela had waked her with an early arrival. Lydia was still in her flannel nightgown, sitting in the rocking chair in her tiny living room. It was easy to see why she would not want to leave the little house to its fate, but obviously she had no real grasp of the danger.

"He's still around," Angela said, "but not with me. And by the way, he's the one who built the dam, and even he's worried about it."

"There's another young man," Lydia went on. "Another friend of yours. He stops in to see me now and then."

"Tom?" Angela could not think who else it might be, and wondered if her grandmother was momentarily confused.

"No, dear, Tom is your brother. I mean the dark one. He goes to New York, and he stops in to see me."

"*Ross?*" She was amazed that Ross even gave a thought to Lydia's existence. "Ross comes here?"

212

"He told me the same thing about the dam. He took me out to show me the water, and he said it's because they're draining it."

She meant the swollen Cat River. It tumbled in a cascade dangerously close to her house.

But in spite of the warnings, Lydia refused to leave. When Angela drove Betty home that night, she appealed to Tom to try again.

He answered, "I'm sure the police won't let her stay there if it really starts looking bad. And I should think there'd be at least a few hours' warning."

"You can't be sure of that. And don't forget, she has no telephone."

Slowly, steadily, the reservoir level dropped. From his field office, Glen watched its progress. If the dam could remain intact until most of the water was drained, then the danger would be over. He thought of the shifting earth. What would make it settle? What if it shifted again? Bastards, why hadn't they seen that the ground was unstable?

No, he should have known. He should have let it settle. Given it more time. That was all he needed now. More time.

He saw a group of people approaching the office. Damned engineers. Consultants. The water people from New York. Day and night they hassled him. As if the dam was his now. He had built it for them, and still they hassled him.

The group was drawing closer. He saw cameras.

He locked the office door and sat down at his desk. When they peered through the window, they saw him talking into the telephone. They knocked at the door, tried the knob and found it locked. He shook his head and waved them away.

They stood outside, besieging him. One even tried to take

a picture through the window, but he reached into a file drawer at that moment, turning his head. In the end, they left. The next day's newspapers reported him unavailable for comment.

La Suisse was busier than usual with crowds of experts, media people, and rubberneckers who came through Burley's Falls to see the dam. Late on Saturday morning, as Angela served a crowd of chattering tourists, she noticed Ross at the entrance. He nodded to her, saw that all her tables were occupied, and met her next to the water pitchers.

"How's it going?" he asked.

"The dam?" She had her mind on Sunday. Glen's deadline. "They're fixing it. They've got three shifts working. Why don't you go and see for yourself?"

"I'm going to. But you stay away from there, Angela. You're safest right where you are."

She was aghast. "Do you really think it might break?"

"Who knows? But don't take any chances. Think of your children."

"Oh my God, Ross, he wants them tomorrow. What am I going to do?"

"Did you tell Tom?"

"He said he'd handle it, but—you know they can take me to court. And Tom's busy with the dam. He—"

"Don't worry about it, Angela. You've got a lawyer. If they take you to court—"

"Don't worry about it!" she exclaimed in disgust. "That's exactly what Tom said. Let the lawyer fight it. What if he fights and loses? Will you please tell me *how* not to worry? Ross, I've got to get back to work."

She was caught in the noontime rush, but it could not stop her from thinking. That night she took three aspirins to help her sleep and woke on Sunday with a feeling of dull dread.

Tom had told her, "If we get backed into a corner, we can always produce the kids."

And then what? There ought to be some way to prove to Glen and his lawyers that the children were safe. Someone who could testify. But then, of course, Glen would know where to find them.

It was seven o'clock. But this was an emergency. She felt no guilt about waking Tom with a phone call.

Betty's worried voice told her that Tom had left for the dam. Only seven o'clock on Sunday morning, and already he had gone.

She phoned her lawyer in Kaaterskill. A telephone answering machine took the message. Later she called Ross's family and was told by his thin-voiced mother that he, too, had gone to the dam.

By ten-thirty, when she had to leave for work, she still had not heard from Glen. She felt a surge of bitter hope. Maybe, if things were happening at the dam, it would keep him busy, at least for a while.

At the restaurant, no one talked of anything but the dam. In awed excitement, they told each other that things were looking bad. And the sky that day was low and gray.

The police had decided on a radio signal. They advised people who lived near the river to keep their radios turned on as much as possible. A few families had evacuated themselves, but general opinion held that an actual disaster was pretty unlikely.

News and rumors crackled all around her, while Angela moved in a fog of her own. She had expected Glen to call her. Maybe he was simply waiting for her to bring the children. And if she didn't?

Were they safe? Could even Tom be sure? She felt a sudden, angry panic.

Betty arrived late and sodden, having had to walk because Tom had taken the car. Angela seized her arm.

"Betty, don't you have any idea where they are? Didn't Tom tell you anything?"

Betty blinked at her, at first not understanding. Then she said vaguely, "Oh—the kids. No, honestly, I don't know. I can have him call you when he comes home. Angela, I'm worried. He's up there working, and what if—"

She stopped at the expression on Angela's face. No one but Tom knew where the children were.

The same thought occurred to Betty. "I should have made him tell me. I'll ask him to write it down somewhere, tonight. If I promise not to look at it. . . . But don't worry. Maybe the person who has them would know to get in touch with you."

"Or maybe they wouldn't."

Betty replaced a fork that had been removed from one of her tables. "Angela, your friend just came in. He's been practically living here. Is he in love with you again?"

"No, it's his daughter," Angela replied. "And the dam. He's keeping track of what happens with the dam."

Ross was on his way back to New York and had come to say good-bye.

"I tried to call you this morning," Angela told him, "but you were up at the dam. Was Glen there? Did you see him?"

"Glen's been holing up there day and night."

"Is it that bad? But they're still draining it, aren't they? Won't it be all right?"

"Let's hope so," he said. "But there's been an awful lot of rain, and the dam wasn't ready to take it all. They should have let it settle in. I've been talking to some of the men."

"But what could they do?"

"Just what they're doing now. Let the water drain out instead of backing up. And I told you, the dam itself isn't sound enough."

"Do you mean—"

"I mean it isn't sound. They've got a lot of repair work."

"Then at least, if he's so busy, maybe he's forgotten about the children. Maybe I have a little more time."

"Yes, I know, That's why—" Ross cut himself short. "I wouldn't worry about the kids. Tom knew this was the day, and he made arrangements. They were at a way station, where he could get them quick enough. Now they'll go back into hiding."

She stared at him, scarcely believing it. "Do *you* know where they are?"

"I didn't say that. Anyhow, Angela, good-bye for now." He clasped her hand. She felt as though, in another moment, he might pull her toward him and kiss her.

"See you soon," he said. "I've got to make a stop on the way and check on my girlfriend."

"Your girlfriend?" She pulled back her hand.

"A relative of yours, down the mountain."

"Oh, my grandmother! Yes, she told me you some-times—"

"Look at that, it's raining again. I'd better get started. I'll see you, Angela. And don't worry. Everything's okay, at least for now."

"Ross, take care!"

Through the window she watched him get into his car and drive out of the parking lot.

She poured coffee for two businessmen, gave her tables a final inspection, and glanced at her watch. It was still early for the dinner crowd.

*　　　*　　　*

217

Bernie O'Connor was exhausted. He had not slept in seventy-two hours. His wife Maggie had pleaded on the phone, "Can't somebody else take over for just a while?" He had to tell her to stop bugging him, they needed to keep the lines clear. They needed—hell, they needed more *time*. There just wasn't enough time, the water was going out too slowly. And that big crack—

"Bernie! Hey, Bernie!"

They were calling him from somewhere. He could barely focus his mind.

"Bernie!"

Ross inserted a tape into his stereo deck. A little *nachtmusik* for driving down the mountain. Not Mozart, but *La Traviata*. He had always liked Italian opera. His father, who used to be a barber, had kept his shop radio tuned to opera whenever he could. Little Ross, playing on the floor among the hair-cuttings, had picked up a taste for it.

Someday, if she was ever free of that arrogant bastard, he would take her to an opera in New York.

He could still hear her voice as she called after him, "Ross, take care!"

Had she guessed? Could she possibly have known why he was stopping at her grandmother's?

"Way station," he had said. She wondered what he meant. It must have been somewhere close by. But how had he known about it at all? Would Tom have confided in Ross?

She straightened a place setting on one of the tables. Refolded a napkin in the shape of a tulip. Rain began to beat against the plate glass window.

She thought of Ross, driving down the road in such a heavy rain. Maybe he would want to get on home and not bother seeing Lydia this time. She could hardly blame him.

218

"Now they'll go back into hiding," he had said. Back into hiding.

There was a sudden commotion in the kitchen. Big Irma came charging through the doors into the dining room.

"This is it! The signal! The police!" She was incoherent. "The *dam!*"

For one quiet, paralyzed instant, time seemed to stretch indefinitely.

Then the dining room erupted. Angela backed against a wall as people rushed past her, talking, shouting, trying to get somewhere, trying to make phone calls.

Flat against the wall. He had said she was safe right where she was.

But there was nothing to be safe from. It hadn't happened. It *couldn't.*

Yet . . .

Lydia. And Tom.

Ross, driving down the mountain. "Ross!" she cried aloud.

He would hear about it on the radio. Maybe Lydia—

Betty ran to her, screaming. "Tom! Angela, he's—"

"They'll get him out," Angela said. "The workmen—they'd be the first to know."

"But he was supposed to get off work. He's on his way home!"

"My grandmother! Did they ever—he said he was—"

She heard Betty inhale quickly and saw the whites of her eyes.

"Where are you going?" Betty cried.

Car keys. She ran to the kitchen.

The staff was clustered around Irma's radio. A reporter's excited voice described what was happening. At that very moment, the dam was giving way. Huge chunks of concrete were tumbling into the Cat, unleashing a deadly tidal wave.

My God, Angela thought, there's no time.

She ran out into the rain. The cold made her realize she had forgotten her coat. It didn't matter. She ran on legs that did not exist.

Her car. She fumbled at the lock.

Betty hurried after her. "Angela, *no*! You'll be *killed*!"

"My children are there!" Angela screamed, and pulled open the door. She turned the key. Nothing.

Nothing. Oh, God, the rain. It was why Florence didn't want the car any more.

Again and again. She would flood the engine. Wear out the battery. Betty hovered in the open door, sobbing.

"Angela, the police—they'll get them out."

She closed her eyes. It had flooded. She could smell the gasoline.

Ross parked next to Lydia's autumn-withered vegetable patch. He found himself whistling "Libiamo, libiamo," as he went to knock on the door. Michael opened it.

"Ready to go?" Ross asked.

"We're having cocoa," said Michael.

"Wait till they finish their cocoa," Lydia called from the living room. "It'll only be a minute. Come on in."

"It's a long way back," Ross said, to hurry them, "and it's already getting dark."

He eased Lydia away from the children. "Mrs. Dawn, the dam looks bad. I wish you'd get out of here for a few days. Go and stay with Tom, or your daughter-in-law."

"What about my chickens?"

"Somebody can bring you down every day to feed them, okay?"

"But I—"

"Listen to me!"

*　　　*　　　*

Thank God, thank God.

She pushed Betty from the door and closed it. Betty ran after her. Angela could hear her voice.

She turned on the wipers. Even then, the rain poured in a steady stream, blurring the glass between wipes. People milled through the parking lot, climbing into cars. She had to pick her way among them with agonizing care. A car pulled in front of her. Viciously she blew her horn. The car lumbered out of the parking lot and turned onto the road that led to Mile Gorge Park. Good God, she thought, only to watch?

From the corner of her eye, she saw the lights in the restaurant go out.

No. Please. Had it reached the power station already?

Of course they would have turned off the power deliberately. But then what about people's radios?

At least Ross, in his car—

And then she remembered. He had no radio. Only the tape deck.

She blew her horn again. Again. People stared at her and scattered from in front of her. She had not known why she was going, only that she had to. Now she understood what had driven her. They wouldn't know about the dam.

The road Ross had taken, the road Lydia lived on, was a steep, winding one that crossed and recrossed the Cat River. Sometimes the Cat ran through deep gorges. Sometimes it dropped many feet in waterfalls. The waterfalls would become avalanches, crushing everything, sweeping up and smashing cars and people as though they were insects.

She had not had time to open the windows. They were beginning to cloud with her hard breathing. Through the steam on the rear window she caught a flash of light.

She had reached the point where the road turned downward. The light flashed brighter. A police car sped up behind her, passed, and turned itself sideways across the road.

No. Not a roadblock.

There was still room to squeeze by. She pressed the gas pedal. A trooper jumped from the car, waving his arms. She blew her horn, flashed on her headlights. As she bore down on him, he stumbled out of the way.

The swerve sent two of her wheels off the road. She felt the car dip, heard the spraying of gravel. She clutched at the steering wheel, waiting to skid. The car flew over the shoulder and bumped back onto the pavement. Through her closed windows came the bellowing of a bullhorn. A sound like a shot.

It couldn't have been. They would not shoot out her tires to save her life.

Then she was around a bend, and safe. Or crazy. Maybe she had been wrong about the children. But Lydia—and Ross—

She glanced at the mirror to see if the police were following, but they had no time to waste on her.

The mountain road became a thread of concentration. It was the only thing that existed. She drove as fast as she could, clinging to the thread, cutting across turns, certain that there would be no other traffic. At every bend she felt a sideways pull as the car tried to flip over.

And then—her first glimpse of the Cat. She saw it cascading down a rocky slide, still only a stream, although swollen with rain and the emergency draining of the reservoir.

Then it was on her other side. She had crossed it. A small bridge, barely noticeable.

When would it come? It couldn't—not that whole reservoir—not where she was.

I'll never make it.

Even if she were to reach Lydia's house, she would never

222

get them to safety. The signal had been ages ago. Never to safety. Now it was too late.

I'm going to die.

She sped on, as though her fate were not a part of what she was doing.

She imagined a wall of tumbling water filled with rocks and trees. A wall, coming down on her. One moment of terror. Like Marcia. Even quicker than Marcia.

Part of her mind raced, thinking of death, while another part concentrated on guiding the car, pushing it as fast as she could without going over the bank.

Ross said, "I'll call Tom when I get home. No, that'll be kind of late. I'll call him from Saugerties. He can come and get you tonight, and then we'll all breathe easier. Your chickens'll be asleep so you can round them up easily." He still thought it ridiculous that she insisted upon taking her chickens. Probably they weren't in any danger. Probably no one was, but he couldn't just leave her there.

"I don't know," Lydia began.

"No more arguments," he said firmly. "Come on, kids. We'll stop at Burger King, okay?"

"I have to go to the bathroom," Michael announced.

"Me, too," echoed Donna.

He closed his eyes and waited patiently. He thought of Katie. Someday he would be taking her, too.

She might not see it coming. Would she hear it? The windows were closed, steaming. She had turned on the defroster. She took her hand from the steering wheel and opened a window, listening. Rain poured in on her. A drop hit her eye. She blinked to see.

She was almost there. Only a few more turns. She had almost made it.

Half of it. Only half. They still had to get back.

She was alone. The only person in the world. This is doomsday, she thought.

Doomsday.

The earth fell out from under her. She screamed, feeling the car spin across the road. And then it stopped, perched on the embankment, its rear wheels sunk in a ditch.

She sat stunned. Then caught her breath. It was not the dam. Not yet. Only ice or oil or just plain water. Or maybe a flat.

The engine had stalled. She turned the key. Again and again, wasting precious seconds. She cried in frustration. Even if she could start it, she would not be able to back it onto the road.

"Help me!" she cried.

The door on her side was pressed against a tree. She would have to slide over. She inched across the seat. The car tipped. She moaned, seeing the sharp drop below her.

And then she wondered: Why not stay here?

But she kept on moving. She could not die without her children. The car tipped again.

It was only settling. Thank God. She pushed open the passenger door and climbed out into the rain. Her throat pulsed, her heart beating high and fiercely.

It was coming—coming. She did not want to hear it. She began to run down the hill.

All around her she could hear the rain. Only rain. But it was coming. Help me.

She ran forever. There was no beginning, no end, nothing but Angela, running. She was soaked and frozen. Rain streamed down her face. And as she ran, she listened.

Any second now. Maybe the radio lied. But it wouldn't. Any second.

And then—the last curve. She could see Lydia's roof. The familiar shingles, brown and green.

And his car! God, his car, still there.

His car. Oh, Ross. . . . Lydia stood beside it. Exhaust poured from the back. He was leaving.

"Ross! Ross! Grandma!"

Lydia turned at the sound of Angela's voice. Angela saw Lydia's mouth open.

She tried to call again. Her breath came hard, as though a knife were in her side. Don't turn off the engine.

There they were, in the back seat. Oh, no—trying to get out. Michael, pushing the seat forward, struggling with the door when he saw her.

She fought the pain in her ribs and screamed, "The dam! The dam!"

Ross gaped at her. Angela reached them, flung open the passenger door and tried to push Lydia into the car.

Lydia went rigid. "I can't go. My chickens. I didn't lock the house. Wait."

"Goddam it," cried Angela, "it's already broken!"

She caught a glimpse of Ross's face, livid with shock. He reached for Lydia's arm. Angela lifted her inside, then squeezed in after her.

Ross's jaw was clenched, his eyes starting. His car faced down the mountain. He spun it around and headed back up to Burley's Falls. The only possible way to safety.

We're going to make it, we're going to make it, she told herself. They had made it this far. They were going so fast— but the curves in the road slowed them down.

Even the children were subdued and tense. She had scarcely paid attention to them as they screeched and chattered at the sight of her. So many months. And now—

"What's going to happen?" Michael asked as they sped,

jolting, up the road. It was all his questions in one.

"We're going to make it," Angela replied. "Anyway, we're together."

The windows quickly steamed. She opened the one beside her. Rain was pouring down, she could hear it everywhere. But when she looked out, it did not seem to be raining hard. Yet the forest echoed with it. Echoed—like thunder—

No. It's coming!

They'd hear it. They would all hear it, the thunder, coming closer. They were flung from side to side as they hurtled up the road, cutting curves, agonizing around bends. The road, the trees, were a blur, and still the thunder came, deafening. It seemed to grow out of the forest.

"Jesus," she heard Ross say.

"Almost there." It was her own voice, but it wasn't true. They would never make it. Too late, she thought. Too late.

Ahead of them, the bridge. Water splashed over the road. She had thought it would come as a wall of water. Instead, the river was swelling at incredible speed. She saw Ross take a breath and hold it. He pressed the gas pedal down to the floor. Force against force. Water splashed through her window. More water pushed against the car, slowing it. She willed them foward. She could see the tension on Ross's face. Forward . . . forward . . .

His hands were clenched on the steering wheel. The water grew and swirled around them. The engine chugged, wavered. It sputtered, then barely caught again.

Were they past the bridge? She couldn't tell, the entire road was under water. She looked back. Water tumbled in a torrent down the slide.

Michael saw her look back. His eyes were huge and frightened. And he had been so happy to see her. He should have stayed happy. They should have had more time.

Water washed about the wheels, growing higher every second. She closed her eyes, clenching her fists.

The car lurched. Her eyes flew open. They would be pushed over the hillside. She did not want to see it—but kept her eyes open so Ross would not be alone.

More water splashed through the window. Water was all around them, pushing, battering, mauling. They were caught. At any moment—

Ahead, through the trees, she saw a light.

A blue light.

"We made it," Ross said in wonder. "We're alive."

Lydia nudged her granddaughter. "If you hadn't come . . ."

Ross eased the car past the police roadblock and stopped. They opened their doors and got out, not minding the rain. "It's only rain," Angela said, feeling it on her face. No one heard her. She did not hear herself. The mountains were roaring as though they would break apart.

The police, in slickers, helped them from the car. She saw the man who had jumped out of her way. He recognized her. Shocked relief was on his face. They all stood in a cluster and listened to the roar. It was the water, scooping up boulders, houses, everything before it. There were sounds like amplified gunshots—the cracking of trees.

She shivered, soaked and freezing. Ross put his coat over her shoulders. They strained to see through the trees. It was all below them, and dusk had fallen.

She saw Lydia's head drop into her hand. Weeping for her home, her chickens. Donna cried, too, frightened by the noise. Michael tried to speak. Angela bent down, and he said into her ear, "What happened, Mommy, is it the dam? My daddy's dam?"

She nodded. The dam he had been so proud of. Michael had never seen it finished. She returned Ross's coat and ushered her children into the car. Ross and Lydia followed, and they drove on into the village.

As they passed La Suisse, she noticed candles burning on some of the tables. A few people moved about, shadows in the faint light.

The power had been cut off all through the village. When they reached Angela's home, they found the house cold and dark. Ross lit a fire in the fireplace while Angela changed into dry clothes. The children followed her everywhere, Donna hugging her legs and Michael demanding an explanation for what had happened.

"*I* would like an explanation," Angela said. "Where were you kids all this time?"

"With Elaine," said Michael.

"My cousin," Ross explained. "Tom said you mentioned New York as a good hiding place. He knew I was there, so he got my number and called me. When you needed a place for the kids, I thought of Elaine. She's divorced, has a couple of kids of her own. It worked out fine."

Michael shook her arm. "Tell me about the dam!"

Angela told him, as gently as she could. "It was a beautiful dam for a while, but it just wasn't strong enough."

Ross said, "I'm going up to look at it next weekend, Angela. I'll take you with me, if you think you can handle it."

"Next weekend! You're not going back to the city tonight!"

"I have a job, remember?" He added ruefully, "I'll have to go the long way around."

Lydia asked, "Where's Florence? And Tom. I want to see Tom."

"Oh, my God, Tom! He was working at the dam!" Angela picked up the phone.

The line was dead. Now she worried about Tom. They put a screen in front of the fireplace and all went out to Ross's car.

The rain had stopped. The clouds were parting. She half expected to see a ruined world. Instead, below them, the forests and fields of the mountainside lay eternal, untouched in the moonlight. The devastation was to the east, concealed behind woods and ridges. They could still hear it in the distance. She wondered how long it would run.

Ross said, "Probably the worst is over."

"Do you think they could ever rebuild that thing?" she asked.

"Maybe. Someday."

She thought of Glen. What would he do now? And the children. No one could take them away again, now that they had been home and seen their mother. Glen might renew—redouble—his efforts, since now he had nothing else. He might even vent his bitterness about the failure of the dam.

They reached Tom's house to find it dark and empty.

"He's not here?" Lydia asked in alarm.

"The Meekers," Angela said, remembering. "Her parents. That's where she leaves the baby when she goes to work."

They drove on, encountering little traffic. The darkened village looked ghostly in the moonlight. Through the windows of the Meeker house they could see candles flickering. In front of the house, half on the road and half on the lawn, someone had parked a dump truck with the words Fabian Construction Co. printed on its door.

"Oh, thank God," Angela cried, knowing it could only be Tom.

Both Betty and Tom rushed to meet them, hugging first Lydia and then the children. Only Tom, besides Ross, had known where the children were that weekend.

"It looks as if we're all in one piece," Tom exclaimed. "How did we do it?"

Ross said, "I'll tell you how. Angela risked her life to come barreling down the hill and warn us. It must have gone just after I left the restaurant.

"And you didn't know?" asked Tom.

"No radio. What about you?"

"We saw it coming. I yelled at the guys to pile in my truck and then I drove like hell away from the dam. By the time we got up high enough, we could hardly see the dam at all, so we came on home the long way around, away from the Cat. We came to Burley's Falls around Kaaterskill way. Most of the guys were from Kaaterskill."

Betty was sobbing with relief and general emotion. Angela asked, "They all got out? You got all the men in your truck?"

He shook his head. "Only the ones who were near me. But the others ran the other way. They must have gotten out. There was time enough for that. All they'd have to do was go up on the bank above the dam. Anywhere above the dam was safe, unless the earth gave way. We'd have stayed, but there was nothing more we could do, and we wanted to get back and look after our folks."

Angela waited, but dared not ask. Tom said finally, "I don't know about Glen."

Lydia decided she would like to stay with Tom and Betty, until, as she added firmly, she could rebuild her house. Ross drove Angela and the children home, where they found Florence, sick with worry until they told her Tom was safe.

Even the relief of knowing their own family was intact did not lessen the horror of the flood. In the next days they learned that twelve people had died. The damage to livestock and property was enormous.

No one seemed to know what had happened to Glen. Neither he nor his car could be found. That led to the opinion that he had simply driven away and disappeared forever, rather than face the consequences of what he had done.

Angela waited for something, some word, although she began to doubt that she would ever hear from him again. Still, the uncertainty tortured her. She kept the children with her and stayed at her job, though there were not many visitors at La Suisse since the mountain road had been washed away.

Three days after the flood, Glen and his car were found in a forest above what had been the reservoir. A revolver was in his hand and a bullet in his brain.

The news of it, to Angela, was sickening and shocking, but it did not really surprise her. She was sure he would not simply have vanished. When the dam was destroyed, Glen was destroyed, too.

The funeral was a lavish one, the last bit of splendor left for Glen, although few people from the area attended. The faithful Stella and Albert were there, Ramona, his cousins with their husbands, and Fay, who still never guessed that Glen might have been responsible for her husband's death. Stanley Morales attended, as did other business acquaintances. And Ross Giordano.

Ross had come, not because of Glen, but to support Angela in the midst of the Fabian camp. Afterward he drove her back to Florence's house.

"I wish you'd get away from here," he told her as she served him coffee in the living room.

"Where would I go?" she asked.

"I know how you feel. This is your place. But it won't be easy for you here. Or the kids, either. You could go anywhere and do anything. You'll have money now, won't you?"

"Yes—whatever I earn. Glen changed his will after I left. The children get some, but not much. He ruined himself building that dam."

"Then what are you going to do? You can't stay at the restaurant forever."

"Why not? Where would I go?" she asked again. "I don't know any other place. Except New York, from that time five years ago."

Ross was silent for so long that she thought he had dropped the subject. Then he said, "All right, if you think you might like to try New York, why don't you come back with me? I'll find you a place to stay."

After some thought, she followed his suggestion. With the children, she moved to New York to begin a new life, far away from the past. Only occasional weekend visits tied them to Burley's Falls and their friends and relatives there.

She was not sure how long she ought to mourn. She waited eight months. Any more than that, she felt, would have been hypocritical. At the end of eight months, she and Ross were married. They had gone a full circle, except that this time they started with a ready-made family of three children.

She often thought of Glen, but not because she missed him. She would think of him and wonder: Would it have been the same even without her predictions? Or would Glen have remained simply Glen, quietly carrying on the family business, with scarcely a thought to taking over the reins in twenty years when his uncles retired?

Was he, as she had once imagined, Macbeth, setting out to make it all happen because she said it would happen, and he believed her? And the others, too. Betty, David, and even Ross. It all started as a game. But they half believed, in spite of themselves. Perhaps she did, too. And their belief made it real.

Sometimes, at night, she would dream of the flood. Her dream did not show the flood the way it really happened. In her dream, the world was a vast lake, and she was in the middle of it. Floating past her, appearing and disappearing in the night, were the people she knew, the ones who had died, and those who were alive. David. Marcia. Tom. Her children. And she was filled with terror and dread.

She never saw Glen in her dream. And she never saw Ross. But she would wake in the bedroom of their New York apartment, and Ross was there beside her. Then her terror would end. The long, long night was over.